Tales of a First-Year Teacher

J.D. Parks

Parks Publishing & Consulting Company, LLC

ISBN -13: 978-1-7326967-0-9

Editing by Jalesa Parks
Front cover image by C.J. Buggs

Print services provided by IngramSpark
United States of America
First printing: August 2018

Published by Parks Publishing & Consulting Company, LLC
P.O. Box 66
Olive Branch, MS 38654
parkspublishingcompanyllc@gmail.com
contact@jdparks.com

Acknowledgements

Most importantly of all, I give all the honor and glory to my Lord and Savior, Jesus Christ, who has been gracious enough to bestow talent and time at my leisure. I could not have completed this novel without His steady hand upon my life.

I must also thank my God-fearing, self-sufficient, and beautiful mother, Melissa Parks, who has offered an undying amount of support, encouragement, patience, laughter, and The Word when I needed it most ----and even when I thought I didn't---it is because of your belief in me that I developed self-confidence and--for a lack of better words----belief in myself. May my future husband be as good to me as you have been all my life. Thank you for inspiring me in ways that only you can. I pray that I am making you proud.

To my Granny, after whom I am named, I appreciate the times that you have spoken positivity over my life and for the endless celebrations where you provided plentiful earthly and, more importantly, spiritual food and didn't rest until everyone had experienced "the fullness thereof" (Psalms 24:1). Thank you for your wisdom and strength.

To my younger siblings---Chelsea, Joseph, and Mia---perhaps the job that I've taken the most serious was being your oldest sister, and you all have made it worthwhile. Thank you for being a sounding board when I encountered roadblocks during the writing process and for listening to my ideas----and even shooting them down. Thank you for entertaining the wild childhood dream I had of becoming a teacher and playing school with me on Saturdays. You all have no idea what you did for me; you've been my greatest teachers.

To my students: being your English teacher was--- and still is--- a blessing. My experiences with you are part of what inspired me to write this book. And in the classroom with you is where I have grown the most, as you managed to keep my feet planted in reality, my nose leveled with the ground, my shoulders squared, and my heart open. I had not experienced such openness until I met you all. And I now understand that true teaching involves the "fruits of the spirit" (Galatians 5: 22-23).My prayer is that other teachers realize what I have come to know, that ALL students far and wide of different skin tones and ethnicities are the most special people in the school, and that without you, the system is broken. I believe that many schools have forgotten you, and that is why they have failed you in so many ways. In the end, I think you just want us to see you, and my dear students, I see you. Thank you for so freely showing yourselves.

To my readers, thank you for giving this book "the time of day." I hope that I do not disappoint you and that you are able to find yourself within.

All my love,

J.D.

Always remember that the head of the fish rots first.

Prologue

Jada watched Mrs. Kimble sashay up to the wooden field house door and peek over her shoulder before making four rapid taps and entering quickly. Jada looked around to see if anyone else was watching. The parking lot was silent and practically empty. Considering that it was close to dinnertime, she was surprised to see Mrs. Kimble still on campus. She sat and pondered on what she should do, tapping her nails against the steering wheel. She could take Mrs. Kimble's word or she could go see if----well--- she didn't know what else she could expect. Other than Mrs. Kimble's consistent visits to the fieldhouse after school hours, Jada had no other reason not to trust her. Yet, Jada found herself exiting her car, gently closing the door, and tiptoeing up to the door. Her chest heaved up and down as she pressed her ear against the door. She could hear scuffles against the floor and muffled noises, and then, it was quiet. Jada pressed her body closer to the door, but there was nothing. She pulled away abruptly, her eyes searching the parking lot. She reached for her phone but realized she'd left it in the car. A loud, guttural moan from behind the door startled her, and she pulled the door handle. The room was dark, with the only stream of light coming from streetlights outside the windows on each wall. Jada's eyes searched the darkness as low moans and heavy breathing permeated the air. Movement on one of the weight benches caught her attention. The half-naked bodies seemed to be entangled, glistening in perspiration, and the hands clawed at skin as if desperate. Jada stood watching as if frozen as the man's hands slowly traveled up the woman's long leg, which he placed on his shoulder just before Mrs. Kimble released a shrill cry. His head fell back and a husky growl escaped from his lips and shook the walls, and Jada saw it. She saw him….

/ *Chapter* One

JADA HARRIS knew that the day she'd met Caleb Moore had just become the second best day of her life. She firmly squeezed the slender bar on the grocery cart, her brown knuckles paling against the steel. Everything seemed to be moving much slower, and she could feel every ridge of stress tumbling from her shoulders and gliding down her two-hundred and thirty-pound frame as squeaking grocery cart wheels, squealing toddlers, and the scent of toasted French bread permeated The Butcher's Shoppe. As she aimlessly pushed her cart down the crowded aisle full of housewives and nursing home veterans, she caught herself smiling for no reason, something that she rarely did. She couldn't believe that Principal Jackson had finally called her back with an official start date, but she could finally relax after two months of relentlessly calling Caldwin High School about available teaching positions. His phone call was exactly what she needed to breathe after months of anxiety. She'd begun to think that moving back home with her mom would be her only option until she'd heard Mr. Jackson's, deep, baritone voice on her voicemail. And now, her nose wrinkled as she thought about her mom's spunky nature and quick-witted comments. They were too much alike; living with her mom just wasn't an option. She exhaled slowly.

Mr. Jackson had said something about things being crazy and intense at the school; she knew that his words would have deterred the average person accepting a mid-year teaching assignment from committing to the job, but she heard his words with anticipation. She was the eldest of four children, who were all raised in a single-parent home, and she currently served as an English instructor at one of Mississippi's most prestigious colleges, there was absolutely no way that a group of obnoxious 14-year-olds could pose a challenge greater than those she had already encountered. She was anxious to whip Caldwin High's 9th grade class into shape. She picked up a box of sirloins so that she could make Caleb's favorite Philly cheesesteak sandwiches for dinner and guided the cart towards the chip aisle, reflecting on what Mr. Jackson's phone call meant: she had a job with her own classroom located near her hometown of Michelin, Mississippi. She couldn't wait to meet her new students, to decorate her classroom in zebra print and blue, and to update her wardrobe. Two Master's degrees later and her hard work was finally about to pay off in a major way! But it also meant that she'd be apart from Caleb.

Grabbing the French bread and a tub of pimento cheese, she thought of Caleb and what the news would mean for them. She'd be moving back home, and Caleb, well, he would be doing what he'd always done: get by. His nonchalance for his career and responsibilities irked Jada beyond measurement, and as of lately, she'd let him know that she wouldn't be staying around much longer just to watch him scrape up pennies for just another pack of Newport cigarettes. She snatched a bag of chips off the rack and threw it in the cart, not realizing that she'd started frowning until an elderly, white woman passed her with a terrified glance. She mumbled an apology and steered her cart down the cereal aisle. Nagging and frown lines had become a part of her normally happy persona, and she didn't like it any more than Caleb, but she couldn't stand to watch him do nothing for himself, or for them. Shouldn't he be pushing her, too? They were so good together at first, opposite of each other in so many ways yet so complementary, but now things had changed. She couldn't shake the feeling that she'd adopted a man-child involuntarily, one who always needed her encouragement and guidance. Quite frankly, she was tired. But ever-so-often there was a sliver of hope. Last night had been the first subtle interaction they'd had in the past six months. She smiled as she thought about their conversation, which had lasted until the early hours of the morning. Stretched out on the couch watching some of their favorite reality shows, he'd gently stroked the kinky strand of black hair that had escaped from her high puff before tipping her face towards him and saying:

"Man, sometimes it's crazy how quickly I fell in love with you. I can see us being married. You know, like *this* all the time, watching our shows and just, you know, being us."

It had caught her off-guard. Not his words but it was the thick sincerity with which he'd uttered them and yet, the feeling that there were still unspoken words on his tongue that made her uncomfortable for some reason. She wanted to urge him to say them, but his dark, soulful pools met her own and beckoned her until their lips met in a fiery storm of long passionate kisses that dropped them on a recluse island flanked by billowing, white clouds and a pinkish sky. This was definitely a pleasant change from the numerous spats they'd been having as of lately. Abruptly, he ended the kiss and shot her a "you-better-stop-me-now" glare that eased into a lazy grin as he rested his hand in her hair and gently pulled her head down to rest on his chest. As he stroked her hair, he sang an offbeat and seemingly remixed version of Chris Young's country song "You." This, she'd remembered, was how they'd met; his difference had drawn her to him three years ago when she was a graduate student working in one of Stockville's local grocery stores.

She had been a front desk clerk lining up packs of Marlboro Lights behind the counter when he'd first entered the store. As he strolled in, she noticed his purposeful stride, and his crisp hairline that flowed smoothly into his mocha skin. His brown eyes seemed to dance, and he breathed a greeting, followed by a slight tilt of his head. Jada returned his greeting with a warm smile of her own before snatching a piece of receipt paper from the cash register and jotting down her cell phone number. Her last relationship had taught her to be more direct along with a few other things that she wished she hadn't learned or felt. She heard her co-worker, Jessica, giggling loudly, and it unnerved Jada to see Caleb (she'd spotted his nametag) at the center of Jessica's attention. Jessica arched her back, exposing her tiny cleavage engulfed in a hot pink and leopard print bra. *Who wears that under a white uniform shirt?* Jada thought. Caleb grinned down at Jessica, and Jada felt the slip of receipt paper crumble in her hand before letting it fall to the floor.

"Um—Jada. Please remember to keep your work area clean." Her manager Mr. Sewell grumbled for the fourth time that day, sweeping the piece of wadded paper into a mini-dustpan that he kept fastened to his uniform trousers.

Jada mumbled a short apology and restocked a carton of Virginia Slims, glancing ever-so-often in Caleb's direction in the mirror above the register. Her chubby cheeks glistened with Vaseline, and she swiped the smudge of eyeliner from her lower lid. She hadn't had time to put on a full face of make-up this morning, but she couldn't help but notice how much happier she looked compared to what she'd seen in the mirror six months ago. Clearly, getting rid of "what's his face" had been the best decision she'd ever made. Her new short, pixie cut had been just the thing she needed to complete her transition from an undergraduate student, to now a single Master's student in Fairfield University's prestigious English program. The cut fit her chubby face and accentuated her dark, almond-shaped eyes, and the auburn highlights gave her skin a nutella-ish hue. She was far from being skinny, but she enjoyed being able to fit into a pair of size sixteen khakis again, ones that she'd long abandoned. Since high school, she'd embraced her plumpness at any size, realizing that being fat was not the epitome of who she was as a woman but rather a gift from God that only the strong could handle. And she'd weathered that storm since childhood. Ultimately, she'd learned that her pants size neither added nor subtracted from her personality. Still, she looked good, and she felt even better! If Caleb couldn't see that she had more substance than Jessica, so be it!

She hadn't heard Caleb approach until he opened the mini-freezer closest to her workstation and deposited a plethora of soda and water. He hummed loudly as he worked with one of the headphones in his ear. She cocked her head attempting to recognize his bad rendition of the song but to no avail.

Frustrated, she asked, "What song is that?"

"Oh, it's Billy Currington's 'Let me down easy.' You like his music?"

"No. I've never heard of him, but obviously, you do."

"Oh, dang. Was I that loud?" He cupped his hand over his mouth, and his eyelids lowered shyly.

"Yeah. I think I lost an eardrum!" She quipped, holding her ears and twisting her face in feigned agony.

"Aww, man. Don't do me like that!" He said with a deep laugh. "You're new here. I'm Caleb." He extended his hand. Jada noticed the veins on his chiseled arm.

She accepted his extended hand. "I'm Jada. "It's just weird to hear a black guy singing country music, and your singing really isn't that bad." She stepped back nervously and slid her hands into her back pockets.

"Oh, you like my singing, huh? I got more!" He began to sing Marvin Gaye's "Let's get it on."

"Whoa!! Let's stop right there!" She held her palm up in protest. "Plus, I'm sure Jessica likes it enough for the both of us." *Why did I say that?!* She silently chastised herself.

"Who's Jessica?" His eyebrows wrinkled in confusion.

I know this little game, Jada thought.

"Oh, come on. She practically jumped in your arms!" She waved dramatically in Jessica's direction. His eyes followed her arms to a smiling Jessica, who smiled and wiggled her fingers at him as she seductively placed film in the printer. "See what I mean? You don't have to play the good guy with me. It's your world. I just live here."

He folded his hairy arms over his chest, giving Jada a thorough once-over as his eyes sparkled in amusement. Jada uncomfortably shifted her weight from one foot to the other and back to the other, silently kicking herself for being so judgmental.

"It's my world, huh?" He said, walking towards her, arms still folded. He stopped just a few inches shy of their chests touching.

She shrugged and turned back to the cigarette rack.

"Well, since it's my world…" He reached around her for the receipt paper loosely hanging from the cash register. His cologne filled her nose as his arm brushed against hers. "Why don't you write your number down so we can talk about that and why I knew your name before meeting you, but I just learned ole girl's name in this conversation with you." He backed away from her, still holding the slip of paper in his hand.

She turned to face him, searching his eyes for any inclination that this was a joke. She found none. Slowly, she grabbed the paper and quickly jotted down her name and number, anxious to tell her mom that she'd found the man she would marry. Later that day, he called, and they had gone on their first date the very same night.

With her in a pair of sweats, since she'd just gotten out of class, and him in his work uniform, they'd laughed as they discussed an Adam Sandler movie they'd watched recently and talked non-stop about their families, past relationships, and future goals. After that, they'd spoken to each other every day; by the third week, they had become exclusive, filling the nights with s'mores over his fireplace, late night hoagies, and midnight movies. And kisses that left Jada panting for more. Before she knew it, months had turned into years, and Jada found herself experiencing a deep affection unlike any other, and she had no intentions of letting it go.

Three years and a bunch of "happy weight" later and she still couldn't believe how different, yet alike, they were. While she was more reserved, assertive, and career-driven, Caleb was passive, impulsive, and he never met a stranger. They'd jokingly exclaimed that in many ways he was the water to her fire. But at the same time, they laughed at each other's jokes when everyone else simply stared back at them in confusion; they shared a strong connection with their families and had both been deeply wounded in former relationships. In essence, they both desired genuine love and had found it in each other. It worked---well---had been working. She checked her phone for missed calls or text messages. Nothing.

I can't believe we haven't talked this morning, she thought. *Maybe I should call him. No, Jay. Give the man his space; he'll call if he wants to talk.*

Hearing the buzz of her phone, she quickly reached into her pocket. Her supervisor needed her to cover one of her colleague's two o'clock English composition courses. She typed a quick, "Yes" and hustled to the self-checkout with her basket of items. It hadn't been the message she'd hoped for, but it was a welcomed distraction. She made a mental note to start purchasing supplies for her classroom tomorrow. Caleb would just have to get in where he fit in.

Chapter Two

The silence between questions irritated Jada. She'd been at the school for at least an hour, and she still hadn't completed a tour of the school. The chubby and stout man sitting across from her seemed more interested in small talk, his lecherous gaze searching her face and raking her body; her leg bounced with impatience as she plastered a fake smile on her face after what seemed to be the fifteenth question.

"I currently teach composition courses at my Alma Mater, Fairfield University, and I've found that many of my incoming freshman struggle with literacy. So, I want to see why and become part of the solution." She smiled stiffly across the table.

"Well, you can't know how excited we are to have you, especially me." The assistant principal's eyes twinkled at her as he shook her hand in a sweaty grip. "And I think that's an honorable cause, Ms. Harris. It is *Ms.*, right?" Jada found his gaze unsettling but shook it off as first day jitters and nodded instead.

"Yes, it's Ms., and I'm happy to be here, Mr. Dennis," she said, her lips slid into a sideways smile. She knew she didn't like him, and she was even more excited to see her classroom. After completing all of the paperwork, she'd felt drained, but, now, walking into the brightly lit lunch room made her feel a bit jumpy.

"So, we'll go this way," he said gesturing toward the B hall of the building. "I'm sure you know by now that we serve a little less than six hundred students, who are about sixty-five percent black, twenty-five percent white, and about ten percent are Hispanic. Something like that----umm---most of the kids are poor and receive free and reduced lunch--oh yeah and just in case you couldn't tell, we just came from the cafeteria." He pointed back towards the long tables they'd just left before turning back towards B hall. "So, there are four halls here. There's A, B, C, and D hall." He pointed towards each space. "Your room is down B hall, so follow me. Oh and I'm sure Mr. Jackson told you that it's 9th grade English you'll be teaching. After the Christmas break, you'll take Mr. Diaz's place, and he'll move to 11th grade English. "

"Mr. Dennis, I would like to know, if you can tell me--- why did the 11th grade teacher leave, and why aren't I being placed in the 11th grade classroom since its empty?"

He stopped abruptly in the middle of the hall. "Oh, I can answer any question *you* have." He grinned at her, as his brown and balding head gleamed through patches of black, wavy hair. "But the teacher was just weak. She couldn't handle the students, and because you're a first-year teacher, we feel much more comfortable starting you with the 9th graders than the 11th graders. I'm sure you'll do great with 11th graders, too, but Mrs. Richmond was a fifth year teacher, and well----you get it. She just didn't fit." He turned quickly and began marching down the hall.

She nodded as her wedge heels clicked against the orange and black, tiled floor. She immediately thought of her youngest sister's comment that her shoes looked like shoes grandmas wear to usher in church on Sundays. She smiled within herself, gazing at the posters that lined the walls. Some announced an upcoming blood drive sponsored by the Beta Club. *Hmmm, so there's a Beta club here. That must be a good sign*, she thought. Other signs promoted a drug-free campus. Finally, they stopped in front of the second to last door on the right. The door was bare, and the window was covered with black paper. Mr. Dennis knocked twice, and a stumpy and pale girl opened the door, frowned at them, and returned to her seat among a large group of girls.

Mr. Dennis entered the room and approached the tidy desk at the back of the classroom with Jada close at his heels. "Mr. Diaz, I want you meet Ms. Harris," he whispered. "She's coming to sit-in on your last two classes and look around if that's okay."

"Oh, fine," Mr. Diaz answered unenthused. "Nice to meet you."

Jada couldn't help but detect annoyance in his voice as his eyes darted nervously around the room. She wondered about his age. The tautness of his tan skin and the blue hoodie he wore gave him the look of a budding thirty-five-year-old, but the gray strands in his curly, black hair and the lines around his eyes said otherwise. Either way, the muscles flexing in his jaw made it clear that she wasn't welcomed here.

"Guh, who she 'posed to be? Michelle Obama?!" one girl quipped.

"Nah, she'en no Michelle. You wouldn't catch her dead in those wedges! Guh, what are those?"

A group of girls in the middle of the room burst into laughter as Jada turned to identify her audience. The first little shoe bully's hair was piled on top of her head in a messy black bun. Her nails were freshly manicured and decorated with bright red rhinestones and her bright red shoes glowed beneath the desk, as she stared back at Jada. She knew she'd found the class loudmouth and jokester who wanted to be seen and felt this was the perfect opportunity to introduce herself.

She strolled over to the group of girls and dropped her bag into one of the empty desks. "Hello, ladies. It's clear that I've caught your attention, and I like to address my fans. I'm Ms. Harris. I'll be your new teacher when you come back in January." She offered the girls a flippant smile. "What are your names?"

The girls blankly stared at her and then burst into laughter. "Mr. Diaz, why you leaving us?!" yelled loudmouth.

"And then the bad part is you leavin' us wit' ha'!" another girl yelled from across the room.

The room erupted into whispers and loud questions and jokes. Jada sat quietly next to the group with the loudmouth and took the time to survey the classroom. The brick walls were covered in gray paint and two large white boards were situated perpendicular to the door. A rectangular window was directly parallel to the door. The room was huge! She was beyond impressed, especially because the school was known for its low scores and student behavior problems, but this room was in great shape. She was even more impressed with the large desks that looked to be practically new, but it all looked too tidy for her, as if it had barely been used. The board to the right of the door was smudged with last week's dates, and the board at the front had personal messages written by students. This unsettled her, and she couldn't shake the feeling that all of the phones on the students' desks were not because they'd been using them for the lesson.

"Okay, okay, guys," Mr. Diaz yelled, interrupting her thoughts and strolling to the front of the room. "I'll still be here, but y'all know Mrs. Richmond couldn't handle the juniors. So, that's where you'll find me. But I'm sure Ms. Harris will be great here. She's gonna sit in with us today. So, let's talk about *Lord of the Flies*."

"Talk about whaaa-?" Loudmouth yelled.

"LaQuira, he talking about the movie we watched!" the same girl yelled from across the room.

"Oh, you talkin' bout the one with them bad kids!" A group of boys laughed.

"Yes, guys and the book we read," Mr. Diaz said leaning against the board exasperatedly. "So, what does it mean to be civilized?"

Looking around the room, Jada noticed the puzzled looks on the students' faces. A group of girls near the door whispered to each other wondering what the word civilized means. The two boys near the desk sat leaned back with their hoods on, cracking jokes back and forth across the room. LaQuira the loudmouth and her group chatted about Mr. Diaz pretending they'd read the book, and the Hispanic group across the room and near the window glanced at their cellphones and talked about the other groups.

Mr. Diaz wrote the term civilization on the board along with its definition as the students continued to look at their phones and pop their fingers. The bell sounded, and they shuffled out of the room, leaving their desks in disarray.

Catching her eye, Mr. Diaz shrugged, and Jada knew she had a lot of work to do.

***

When the school dismissal bell rang, Jada pressed two fingers to her right temple as the students ran down the halls. To say that she'd seen enough in one day was an understatement. The last class had been much more energetic. They were eager to get out of their seats, and although they'd been much less vocal about losing their beloved English teacher, she could still feel their resistance to her. She'd introduced herself to the whole class and sat quietly as the remainder of the class played out very similar to the first one she'd observed. She had recorded pages of notes geared towards altering negative behaviors she'd witnessed. Her first order of business would be creating a strong policy against cellphones and for appropriate classroom decorum. These were just two of the items on her rather extensive list---one of her many lists.

"So, how'd it go, Ms. Harris?" She jumped at Mr. Jackson's voice. He wore a bright pink sweater vest with a lime and white striped collar shirt. His pants were lime green and crisply starched, and his brown leather loafers sparkled against the tile. *What a combination,* she thought.

25

"Oh, everything went well. They have a lot of energy that I'm not used to, but I think I can put it to good use." She struggled to keep up with his long strides without losing her breath.

"Yeah, I'm sure you will, but next week is finals week and then Christmas break. All teachers return back on the fourth of January and the kids come back on the fifth. So, make sure you're here bright and early on the fourth in the library at 8:30. Here's the key to your classroom, so if you want to come in early in January and set up your classroom just let me know, and I'll have someone unlock the building for you. If you have any questions just call or shoot me an email, okay?" Jada nodded as the overload of information swirled in her head, and she accepted his extended business card and the key to her classroom. "Welcome to the Beagle family." He patted her arm and walked swiftly in the direction of the main office.

"Oh, Mr. Jackson," she called. He turned slowly. "What about the textbook? Can I get a teacher's copy today?"

"We only have classroom sets. Come see Ms. Allen, and she'll get you squared away." She followed him into the office. "Ms. Allen, can you get Ms. Harris a teacher's edition of the 9th grade English textbook?" The secretary popped her gum and shot Jada a fake smile

"Thank you, Mr. J-" she was cut short by his cell phone ringing. He held up his finger, answered the ringing phone, and shuffled to the back of the office, throwing up his hand in farewell. Jada turned her attention to the petite, brown-skinned receptionist who was eyeing her from the kinky curls on top of her head to her low wedge heels. The woman sucked her teeth and yanked the glass window open that separated her from Jada and the waiting area.

"I could've sworn that I am the receptionist, not the librarian. Next time, you need to go to the librarian for all book needs. What book you need again?" The woman snapped at her.

Jada bit her tongue. "The teacher's edition of the 9th grade English textbook," she managed to mumble through gritted teeth.

The woman busied herself looking through the numerous cabinets and drawers. "How long you say you been teaching?" she asked, peeping over her pink glasses.

"Oh, I've never taught in a public school if that's what you're wondering."

The receptionist seized her rummaging. "Hmph. Never?" She swiveled around to peer at Jada. "Honey, that last teacher quit, and she had been a teacher for five or six years." She dropped the thick, green textbook on the countertop on the other side of the glass. "Good luck, new booty." She whipped a lipstick tube and compact mirror from her designer bag and began to slather the hot pink paste along her chapped lips. "Mm-hm. These kids some serious, and the teachers, too." She yanked the glass window closed with a loud thud.

"Wh-" Jada's phone rang. It was Caleb. She murmured thank you to the receptionist. "Hey, babe." She answered, walking to her car with the phone tucked in the nook of her neck.

"Hey, baby. How'd it go?"

"Well, it's certainly different from college. The little girls have attitudes, and they already hate me. I'll have to get that in check. Plus, the teacher pretended that they'd read *The Lord of the Flies*, but it was clear that they'd only watched the movie " She opened the door to her gold PT Cruiser, throwing the textbook on the passenger seat before settling behind the wheel. "But the school itself is nice on the inside. You can tell that it's been remodeled recently and that the janitors seem to take care of the halls and stuff. My classroom is huge, but I gotta decorate because right now, it's pretty boring and dead." Silence. "Caleb, you there?" She pulled the car onto the expressway back towards Stockville.

"Yeah, babe. I'm here. I'm glad you like it, and I'm sure you'll get their bad tails into shape. But babe, I still don't see why you couldn't just stay here in Stockville with me and teach college. You like teaching here, right?"

Jada rolled her eyes and blew into the phone. They'd already had this conversation many times. "Caleb, you know I like teaching there, but like I've told you, it's more money and experience. I'm trying to see what's goin' on in public schools. You act as if we live together, and I'm leaving you with bills or something. Like, it's bad enough that we've been together almost four years, and you still haven't gotten yourself together. I can't plan my life around someone who doesn't want anything."

"Here you go with that again. Forget I said anything, okay? Just let me know when you get close."

"But I wasn't fini----." The line went silent as he ended the call. "Thanks for really listening to my day," she mumbled, tossing her phone onto the passenger seat and pressing the gas pedal harder as Lee Ann Womack crooned loudly from the speakers.

"What were those kids talking about? There was no helicopter in the book!" She yelled to no one in particular.

Chapter Three

Duchess was everything a pet owner didn't want. Attitudinal. Feisty. Unfriendly. Nosey. Lazy. And temperamental, but Jada couldn't think of a better cat. When Jada had visited the animal shelter, she'd sensed something about the cat that no one else did and had adopted her the same day. To say that she'd grown attached to the patchy gray and black fur ball would be an insult to the feline's one-of-a-kind attitude. Duchess lounged lazily on top of the refrigerator as Jada scrubbed the countertops.

"When I get ready to mop, you're gonna have to go to your kennel, missy." She said glaring at the cat that seemed to return her stare with one of defiance.

She'd spent the whole day packing up her one-bedroom apartment. She remembered the feeling of accomplishment and pride she'd felt when she'd purchased her kitchen table set for thirty-five dollars from a random guy on Facebook. She'd felt even more accomplished when she, along with Caleb, had picked up furniture from her grandmother's house, driven to Michelin to get her bed, and carried everything into the apartment for set up. It felt unreal to think that in two days she'd be graduating and moving back to Michelin, leaving everything she'd known for the last six years behind.

Just then, she felt Duchess wrapping her furry body around her ankle. "You have your sweet moments, huh, Duch?" She picked her up and settled onto the couch. "We're moving to a new place, girl." Duchess jumped down and strolled to her litter box. "Hmmmph. Tell me how you really feel." There was a knock at the door. Her mother stood on the other side in a brown shawl with large brown boxes in her arms.

"Hey, Ma!" She yelled opening the door wider and enveloping her mother in a long bear hug. The boxes clattered against the floor.

"Hey, my Jade." Her mother's eyes sparkled with pride at her oldest daughter. She couldn't believe that all her talk about finishing school and being an example had actually worked, but she was glad it did. Now, she had a daughter with two Master's degrees, and she knew that her younger children had no choice but to follow suit. She dragged her stuffed suitcase into the apartment as the others shuffled up the steps.

"Jay!" Her youngest sister Selena yelled, rushing towards her as her other sister and brother entered the small apartment. "We're starving!"

"Hey, y'all! I would've asked if ya'll needed help, but I was sure you had it." They all rolled their eyes before plopping down on the couch. "So, I was thinking that I'd just order pizzas 'cause Caleb is on his way over, too. Cool?"

"Cool," her brother Julian answered for everyone. Seeing her family sprawled all over the living room made her tiny apartment feel more cozy and complete. She enjoyed seeing them so comfortable and relaxed in her space. Even Duchess seemed to be relieved to see them.

Everyone I love in one place, she thought, looking for the menu and the deck of cards.

***

"I have no idea where he is," Jada sighed, checking her phone for what felt like the millionth time.

She couldn't believe Caleb hadn't showed up to help her load her stuff into the U-Haul and see her off. Yesterday, as she took pictures in her cap and gown and surrounded by her family, he'd seemed out of place and uncomfortable. She knew he was still upset about her leaving but not to this degree. Out of the corner of her eye, she could see her mom fuming with impatience and disappointment.

"Jade," her mom started. "I don't think he's coming. So, we'll do what we've always done----handle it ourselves." Too numb to speak, Jada nodded her head in agreement, as her siblings began picking up large boxes and marching towards the U-Haul truck. She watched in amazement, as her mom commanded the room, and soon, only the couch and mattress set were left.

"Jada, get on the other end of the couch."

"Ma, me and Jules can get the couch. I don't want you to hurt yourself."

"Little girl, who do you think was carrying in the couches and stuff before you. I was. Sometimes, if you wait on a man, you'll be waiting forever." She winked at her. "Now, let's go."

Jada placed her hands under the long couch, but a cardstock piece of paper rubbed her fingertips.

"Hold on, Mom." She pulled out a purple and pink flowered birthday card. Caleb had given it to her. She opened it to the generic words of love that adorned every card, and she remembered how upset she'd been to find that he'd spent eight dollars on a card, without adding any personal words of his own.

Her mother's voice invaded her memory, "Jada, we need to get going."

She quickly wiped an escaped tear from her cheek. "Okay, mom. Let's go." They slowly walked the couch down the stairs and into the U-haul truck, followed by the mattresses and bed frame. As they walked up the stairs, the familiar sound of an engine popping and wheels whirling floated into the apartment complex. She watched Caleb unfold his long body from his father's old, silver coup, with an embarrassed smile. He strolled up to her, not saying a word. She stared at him before turning and walking into the apartment, her shoulders high and back straight in annoyance.

"Caleb's here, guys," she announced.

"So, you finally decided to show up, huh?" Her brother greeted him, slapping him on the back.

"Yeah, man, I overslept." His explanation was met with silence. "Okay, so let's get the mattresses."

"We already packed up everything." Her sister, Cara, offered dryly.

Wow. You guys work fast."

"Yeaaah. That's what it is." Selena drawled sarcastically.

"Okay, ya'll," her mother interrupted. "Let's get this place scrubbed down and vacuumed, so we can get out of here."

Caleb grabbed the vacuum cleaner, while Jada and the others worked to scrub down the kitchen and bathroom.

An hour later and she placed the key on the countertop, turned off the light, and closed the apartment door.

Caleb stood at the bottom of the stairs awaiting her. "You know, you really don't have to leave, right?" He brushed an eyelash from her cheek before placing his hands in his pocket and rocking back and forth on his heels, a puff of smoke forming in the cool air.

"I do have to leave. I've accomplished what I came to do. There's nothing left here for me." She rubbed her gloved hands together.

"What about me? I'm here." He peered into her eyes.

"Yeah, you are here. You've been here all your life. I've been here with you for three years, and nothing has changed, Caleb."

"Is this because I showed up late today?"

She scoffed, "No. But that sure didn't help. Don't act like this is new. Today was just another example of how I can't depend on you, even for the small things. Like, I booked the U-Haul; I went and gathered most of the moving boxes. All you had to do was show up, and you couldn't even do that." She raised her hands towards the sky. "That was all I asked you to do----show up." She stared back at him.

"Jada, it's just furniture. Don't make this bigger than what it has to be." He kicked a windblown stick into the grass.

"I'm not. I don't think you get it." She crossed her arms and stared at the sky. "You want me to be here with you, in a home three doors down from your family, playing house, and embracing the country life. You don't even have steady income. I don't want you on your terms. You'll be happy, and I'll be miserable."

"I'll make sure you're not miserable. Trust me." He stepped up to her, his chest touching hers. He tucked her jet black hair behind her ear, his signature gesture. "I love you; can't you just trust me?"

The smell of his cologne and his sudden closeness broke her resolve. The last thing she wanted to do was leave on bad terms. She kissed his lips softly. "I love you, too. But love is not enough now. It's just not." She brushed past him and yanked down the U-Haul door before turning back to him. "I'll miss you," she said softly.

"I'll miss you more, man, but I'll try to visit as much as I can. You know money's tight right now." He pulled her into a long hug before walking her to the oversized truck and opening the driver side door. "You be careful." She could see the emotion glistening in his eyes, but she couldn't afford to give in to it right now.

"You know it." She pecked him on the cheek one last time before climbing in, cranking up the truck, and giving her mom a thumbs up. They pulled out of the complex, leaving Caleb standing in the middle of the parking lot and blowing cigarette smoke, his eyes fastened on the ground. As she watched his form shrink in the side view mirror, Jada swept the tears away as they fell, wishing he'd given her a reason to stay a long time ago.

Chapter Four

"We are so glad to have three new faculty members here with us at Caldwin High School. Let me introduce you to Mr. Harper, who will be teaching economics." Jada watched a tall, muscular man stand and give a slight wave before returning to his seat. "Mr. Harper, we're so glad to have you," Mr. Jackson greeted him with a warm smile. "Next, we have Mr. Vincent, who will be teaching art. He will also drive one of the busses for us. I'm sure many of you know him since he's Caldwin High alum." The faculty clapped and hooted as Mr. Vincent smiled goofily, stood, waved, and quickly returned to his seat. "Lastly, we have Ms. Harris, who recently received two Master's degrees in English and education. She will be teaching 9th grade English for us."

Jada stood, smiled, and gave a quick wave as the faculty clapped. She noticed that a group of women sat whispering and eyeing her. The two coaches, Coach Lewis and Coach Young, who had escorted her to Mr. Dennis' office the first time she visited the school, slapped each other on the knee. She couldn't help but feel uneasy as she watched their exchange.

"Ms. Harris, we're really glad to have you here as well." Mr. Jackson cupped his hands in front of his torso. "Okay, family, we need to come back to school this semester, even stronger than before. The kids are gonna come back from Christmas break, and they will be dragging. Now, don't get me wrong, they'll be talkative and excited, but it won't be about getting to class. So, after talking with Mrs. Kimble and Mr. Dennis, we decided to start a hall competition."

Murmurs erupted around the room. "We ain't got time for no competition," one teacher whispered to another.

"I hope I'm gettin' money for this lil' competition," another murmured.

"I still gotta work on my classroom," a teacher from the back hissed.

"Whoa, whoa. Wait, guys. I know you have a lot of questions, so hopefully, after I finish, I will have answered them all." Mr. Jackson pointed the laser pointer at the large projector screen. Four quadrants in different colors popped up on the screen, each quadrant labeled with a letter from A to D. "One of the main things I want to cut down on this semester is the number of students lingering in the halls after the tardy bell. We have entirely too many students in the halls, without passes, and Mr. Dennis has very few referral slips for tardies, which doesn't make sense. It tells me that many of you are allowing students to come in after the tardy bell has rang; therefore, you are not holding them accountable. I'm not too proud to ask for your help, and I, well, we, need your help."

Jada was in awe of his humility. Looking around the room, she wasn't alone. Mrs. Kimble, the Chemistry teacher and Cooking Club sponsor, sat smiling at him in admiration, with her long, brown legs crossed at the knee. Her pointed toe, stiletto shoes bounced up and down in the stream of light from the projector. She turned suddenly, her long hair falling in front of her eyes, as she stared back at Jada. Embarrassed that she'd been caught, Jada attempted a small smile; Mrs. Kimble turned her attention back to the screen.

Mr. Jackson continued, "Okay, so on the screen, you see quadrant A; this represents hall A. Quadrant B represents Hall B. Do we get it?" His question was met with murmurs of agreement. "Great. So, between each class, the principals and Ms. Calloway will stand watch to see which hall has the least amount of students in the hall at the sound of the tardy bell. At the end of the nine weeks, the hall with the lowest count will receive dinner on us. Does that sound good?"

Many of the teachers hooted, and some clapped. Others began to murmur and whisper about keeping track of tardies.

"We got more important things to worry about."

"Just another job that we don't get paid for."

"They only want us to make their jobs easier."

"Watch. When all those referrals roll in, they'll try to come up with something else."

Jada was confused. She didn't know whether she should be upset about the competition or excited. She found herself being the latter. It couldn't possibly be as big of a deal as they were making it out to be. Plus, she liked healthy competition.

"Now, the policy is still the same. After three tardies, write their behinds up and send it to the office. No exceptions. We will handle it from there, but you must complete the referral form to cut down on confusion. That way when the parent comes up here ranting and raving about their child receiving suspensions or detention, we can pull out the referral slips as documentation, but if we don't have them, it becomes a battle of your memory versus that of the child. We don't want that. So, Ms. Calloway is coming around now with referral slips that have been updated. Throw out the pink ones from last semester."

Ms. Calloway, a tall, slender middle-aged woman with caramel skin and long, poofy hair gathered a stack of the slips and strolled from table to table, dropping smaller stacks onto each one. She didn't strike Jada as being very friendly, as she plopped a stack on their table without uttering a word. Jada knew that she was the instructional facilitator, but she couldn't figure out why she would be updating the discipline forms.

"We wanna thank Ms. Calloway for making the necessary changes to the form so that it is more user friendly for you all." Many chuckled at his attempt to crack a joke. "Ms. Calloway, do you have anything you want to say about these forms?"

"Yes, Mr. Jackson, thank you." She strolled to the front of the room. "I hope these are much easier to use than the other ones that Mrs. Taylor made before she decided to just up and leave in the middle of the school year. And like, if you have something to say about them, don't take it to Mr. Jackson or go talk about 'em to the next teacher. Come tell me. A closed mouth doesn't get fed." She intertwined her fingers in front of her stomach and stood stoically, taking a few seconds to stare down each table. "Okay, if there are no questions, I'll turn it back over to you, Mr. Jackson." She strolled back to her seat.

"Thanks again, Ms. Calloway." Mr. Jackson jogged to the front of the room. "Once again, I think I speak for all the administrators when I say that we appreciate all of your hard work and dedication to our students here. Being a teacher is not an easy task, but to give you a bit of motivation, I would like to show you a clip from *Facing the Giants*. As you watch this scene, I'd like for you to think of ways that you can further encourage our students to excel." He pointed at

Mrs. Dixon, the school librarian, who started the clip and lowered the lights.

Jada was captivated by the clip and the coach's tenacity as he pushed the self-defeated team captain to complete the extraneous death crawl while holding one of his teammates on his back. *Yes,* Jada thought. *This can be me; I can push these students and get them out of this small town. I can do this.* The sudden stream of light interrupted her thoughts.

"See, guys. This is what teachers do," Mr. Jackson offered quietly. "We encourage, nurture, challenge, defend, protect, and yes, we love our students. I expect nothing less. Let's finish out the school year strong. Are there any questions?"

The room was silent.

"Okay, if there are no questions, please pick up a revised bell schedule, bus and game duty assignments, and a class inventory form. You're free to work in your classrooms until three, and then, you'll be free to leave. Meeting adjourned."

Jada watched as the teachers hurriedly filed out of the room, chattering loudly. As Ms. Calloway walked past, Jada called out to her.

"Yes?" she answered with a tone of annoyance.

"I know that you're the instructional facilitator, so I was wondering if there is a protocol when it comes to composing lesson plans? Also, is there a school-wide pacing guide? I'm not quite sure if I'm asking the right questions." She chuckled nervously.

Ms. Calloway answered stiffly, "No, there are no lesson plans or pacing guides. I don't really check them. When I come in to evaluate you, I just need to be able to tell that the students aren't just sitting there. Diaz didn't teach squat, so it won't be hard to do better than him." She chuckled.

"Oh, um, okay," Jada said, not quite sure what to make of her words. "Thanks."

The woman pranced away so swiftly that Jada wondered if she'd ever been there. She couldn't shake the feeling that she hadn't received appropriate answers for her questions and that Ms. Calloway hadn't seemed concerned enough to help.

"Hi, there!" Jada felt a firm tap on her shoulder. She turned to see a slender, chestnut-colored man, with a small black afro. His glasses seemed to be securely fastened to the tip of his nose, and she could see his pink collared shirt nestled snugly under a dark green pullover.

"Hi, I'm Jada" She stuck out her hand.

"Oh, come on now, I hug." He gripped her hand tightly and pulled her into a firm embrace. "I'm Mr. Williams; it is like sooo nice to have you here with us!" He released her reluctantly, still holding her hands, with his face mere inches from hers.

This guy is all up in my personal space, she thought. His friendliness was a bit off-putting.

"What's your Alma Mater?" He released her hand and crossed his arms over his chest, concerned lines accented his forehead.

"Fairfield University. What about you?" She shifted her work bag to the other arm and attempted to put a few spaces between them.

He pushed his glasses up on his nose and took a step towards her. "Oh, Booker T. Washington University, you know the HBCU. I graduated top of my class and pledged Phi Delta Rho," he said, cupping her elbow.

I just can't get away from this guy. She readjusted the strap of her bag on her shoulder, causing his hand to loosen her elbow.

"Did you pledge?" he asked expectantly.

"I did, Mu Gamma Rho," she replied.

"Ooooo, a Rho after my own heart." His hand grazed her shoulder. "I just want to welcome you to Caldwin High. I teach Social Studies down Hall C. So, if you need anything, like the school gossip, news, a shoulder, or anything, you are more than welcome to visit my classroom. It's the one with the red, purse-shaped tape dispenser on the desk." He winked at her before quickly exiting the library. Jada couldn't help but wonder if he'd been skipping as he left.

"Thanks, Mr. Williams!" she called after him.

He offered her a tiny wave and disappeared around the corner. She made a mental note to tell Caleb about him, but for the time being, she had a lot of work to do. She hustled to her classroom, ignoring the lustful gaze of Coach Young from the back of the library.

Chapter Five

"Where'd this freaking train come from?" She wondered aloud to no one in particular. It was the first official day of class, and the train moved at buggy pace in front of her. As many times as she'd drove past the school, she'd never encountered a train. Luckily, she had given herself more than enough time to set up and walk through her classroom before the students were allowed to enter the building at 7:45.

Tapping her unpolished nails against the steering wheel, she thought about Caleb. She had talked to him briefly yesterday, but after she'd told him about her day, they'd had little more to talk about. The tension was thick as she asked him about his family, and he answered in short sentences. She knew he was still upset and resorted to rushing him off the phone. She knew she wouldn't talk to him today.

The blaring of the train's horn pulled her from her thoughts just as the train stopped and proceeded to move in the opposite direction it had been going.

"Oh, come on!!" she yelled, slapping the steering wheel.

"This is ridiculous!"

Her phone buzzed in the passenger seat. It was her mom.

"Hey, Mama." She was grateful for the distraction.

"Hey, I told you to call me when you made it, little girl."

"Oh, yeah, but I haven't made it yet. I'm stuck on the other side of the train."

"Oh, no, and I know how impatient you can be, but good, you have time to talk to an old woman."

"Always," Jada smiled into the phone.

Out of everyone, her mom had been the most consistent, never wavering from her beliefs and keeping a close eye on everyone in the family. It had been harder for some of Jada's friends and even her boyfriends to understand the relationship she had with her mother, but it had also been hard for them to grasp a single mother sending all of her children to college, and yet, it had been Jada who never asked anyone for money or a ride to the store. Now, it was still her mother calling to check on her before the first day of teaching.

Without a doubt, her mother weighed heavily on her heart, and she didn't care if anyone understood it.

"So, are you nervous?" Her mother asked.

"Well, yes and no. I'm not exactly sure what to expect. I heard so much yesterday that I'm kinda wondering if I'm up for the challenge. Can I really handle these kids?" Her voice rose as she peeped the end of the train nearing her.

"Jade, what I have I told you? We're Harris's. We don't take anything from anyone. These are just children. You have commanded my house for years as the oldest child," she chuckled. "There is absolutely no reason that you can't do the same for these children. Just don't let them run over you, and remember that with every step you take, God has you. Do you hear me?"

"Yes, Mama. I hear you." Jada fought back a tear that had formed in the corner of her eye. "Thank you, Mama. You always know what to say."

"I'm the Mama. I know my children." she chuckled. "Feel better?"

"Yeah, I do actually. And you got me through this train, too," she heaved an exaggerated sigh of relief.

"Good. Now, call me if you get the chance. Better yet, just text me throughout the day to let me know you're okay, okay?"

"Okay, mom." She sped across the railroad track.

"Alright, love you baby."

"Love you, too." She ended the call and turned into the school's parking lot.

The American flag floated high above the school building as students ranging in age strolled to wait in front of the school. Following one of the school buses, she drove to the back and parked in front of the football field. Being that she was forty-five minutes early, she wasn't surprised to find three other cars already parked behind the school. She glanced at herself in the mirror, reapplied her lipstick, and stepped out of her car. She couldn't help but notice that the black Tahoe parked one parking space away from her was still running, and the windows were foggy. Her anxiety subsided when she noticed the faculty tag hanging from the rearview mirror. She shrugged off her apprehension, grabbed her bag from the backseat, and marched into the building with her rolling briefcase bouncing on the concrete behind her.

***

"I'm Ms. Harris. Please take a syllabus and pass the rest back." She stood in front of her first period class, stopping at each row to count and distribute papers for the row. "Do you all know what a syllabus is?"

Her question was met with silence, as some students stared blankly at her, others peeked down at their phones, and a few placed their heads on their desks.

"Well, since no one seems to know, let me tell you that it's a guide for the rest of the year. It tells you everything you need to know about the class, like what we'll be doing from week to week, the rules and regulations, how I will grade your assignments, everything." She smiled. "Now, let's walk through the rules. The first one is that until I learn your names, you must sit in assigned seats."

Grunts and moans filled the room.

"Calm down. Once I learn your names, you can sit wherever you'd like. That's the deal." She smiled. "Now, let's move. I need Penelope Barnes in seat number one." She stood beside the desk, waiting for the unenthused little girl. She was fair-skinned with a nose ring and blue hair. From her dark clothing, Jada assumed that she was into Goth or emo style. "Hi, Penelope." The girl nodded in acknowledgment.

"Next, let me have Christina Clark." She moved towards the second seat in the first row. A tall, slender, mocha-toned girl stepped forward to reclaim her seat. "Hi, Christina," she greeted. The girl offered a meek and low-toned greeting before returning her attention to her phone.

"Then, we will have Mr. Ashton Gross." She peered at the group of remaining students. A tall and somewhat chubby boy jumped from behind the others.

"Yooo, that's me, Ms. Harrisy." He folded his hands into a tight fist in front of his chest, as if he were a rapper that had just spoken the best bars known to man. "You heard that? Me and Harrisy? Rhyming. You liked that, huh?" He flashed a goofy smile, as the others giggled behind him.

"Ummm, yes, Ashton, very clever." she said, giving him a blank stare. "Can I get you to take the third seat for me?"

"Sure thing!" He hopped over the desk and flopped into the seat.

"Okay, next, Demetria Herman?" She glanced around the room.

"Oh, she probably ain't coming today," Ashton offered. "She hardly ever come to school nowadays."

"Okay, thanks for telling me, Ashton," she made a note beside the girl's name. "Does anyone possibly know why she doesn't come?"

The students shot glances at each other across the room. They seemed to be silently asking each other for permission to answer the question before averting their eyes to the floor.

"Nah," Ashton said dryly. "We don't know why she not comin'"

"Oh, okay," Jada made an additional note to inquire about the student later. "Let me have Varnisha Lloyd and Jose Mendez now." The two students stepped forward. "Varnisha, you can take seat number five, and Jose please take number six." They scurried to their seats.

"Vanessa Pigues for seat number seven, please." The girl dragged to the seat, with her furry hood hanging low and covering her face. "Vanessa, please remove your hood."

"I always wear my hood," the girl snapped back. "Don't try to come up in here and change stuff just 'cause you new. I ain' new; we been here." She leaned back in her seat, the slit of her eyes showing beneath the rim of the hood.

"That's nice to know, but part of being respectful is allowing your teacher and classmates to see your face when you talk to them. I'd hate to make an example out of you on the first day back, so remove your hood."

The girl smacked her lips. "You just gon' have to make one outta me today." She blew a large bubble and sucked the gum back into her mouth before staring into her phone.

"Alright, Miss Pigues, please step outside the classroom."

Many heads left the desk and fingers stopped pecking on phones as the girl noisily gathered her belongings, stormed out of the classroom, and slammed the door.

"Mane, foo', wildin'" Ashton chuckled.

Jada finished assigning seats and introduced the students to their first quickwrite assignment: What would you like to accomplish, experience, feel, and change as a student in this class? As they worked, she stepped out into the hall.

Vanessa was seated on the floor against the wall. She didn't look up as Jada approached her.

"Vanessa, can you stand up please?" Jada stood near her, her hand still clutching the classroom door.

"No."

"Can you tell me what's going on? You know the school's dress code doesn't even allow hoodies, and all I'm asking is that you lose the hood. Why do you want to keep it on in class?"

Silence.

"Okay, if you don't tell me something, anything, I will have to write you up."

"Look, I don't know you like that. I'll take the write up." The girl pulled out her phone and a slender tube of lip gloss before applying a thick layer as she looked into the phone's camera.

Jada knew that in order to establish her rapport as a no-nonsense teacher in the school, she would have to make an example. She opened the door, pushed the office call button, grabbed one of the referral forms from the back of the door, and proceeded to complete it. The other students began to murmur but stopped when she glanced up from the form.

"What we got, Ms. H?" Coach Lewis drawled as he approached her.

"It's Harris," she shifted uneasily in her pointed-toe flats. "And I already called the office." She waited for him to retreat. Much to her surprise, he leaned on the wall, placing his hand above her head. She shifted from under the arch of his arm.

"Ms. Harris, I have a degree in administration, so many office calls are referred to me." His front, fake tooth glistened beneath the ceiling's fluorescent lights. His grin was unsettling.

"B-b-but, don't you have a class right now, too?" she stammered.

"Yeah, but they're doing some book work." He looked her up and down. "Now, the sooner you tell me what happened here, the sooner I can get out of your hair." There was that grin again.

Jada wondered how he managed to assign book work on the first day back but decided not to ask about it. "Um, okay, well, Ms.

Pigues here refused to remove her hood while in class, so I asked her to step out and explain it to me, but she refused to do that, also." She glanced at a seemingly bored Vanessa still sitting on the floor, now twirling a long strand of hair that had escaped from under the hood.

"Get up here, girl," Coach Lewis spat. She stood slowly. "What's your problem, huh? You're too pretty to be acting like this. Do I need to talk to Coach Young about you?"

The girl's eyes widened and quickly darted down the hall as she shook her head profusely. "N-no, sir," she stuttered nervously.

Jada was surprised by the girl's sudden change. For some reason, it troubled her.

"I didn't think so." He said. "Now, you get in that room and do as Ms. Harris tells you. You understand?"

"Y-yes, sir." She began walking toward the door.

"Take the hood off now!" he yelled.

She quickly snatched the hood off and escaped into the classroom.

Amazed, Jada asked, "So, who is Coach Young to her?"

"Oh, she's one of the sped students. You should've received an IEP folder for her. Did you get any folders?" She shook her head. "Well, they should be coming soon. She has a lot going on at home plus she has other learning disabilities. Coach Young is her sped teacher for Social Studies, and since she came to the high school, he's really been working close with her to keep her on track. So, if you have any other problems with her, try speaking with him first."

Jada nodded slowly. "Okay, great. Thanks for your help."

"Anytime, lady." He pushed off the wall, gave her a quick salute, and strolled away.

Entering the classroom, Jada noticed that many of the students' papers were blank, and their cellphones sat in their laps.

"Okay, ladies and gentlemen, let's talk about rules number two and three." She stood in front of the classroom. "Cellphones are not allowed. All of them should be put away right now." She watched as some students hesitantly placed their devices in their backpacks or purses, and others seemed to be contemplating challenging her. Eventually, all desks and laps were clear. "Next rule, you are to complete all assignments or receive a zero. So, I just gave you assignment number one. I'm going to go grab my gradebook, come around and check to see who did it, and then, I'll have you share it aloud."

As she strolled to her desk, she heard papers rattling as some students struggled to find paper to complete the assignment. Others murmured their disapproval. Passing Vanessa's desk, she noticed multiple lines on the girl's left arm that appeared to be scratches peeking out from under her royal blue coat. Jada grabbed her gradebook and made a note to check into it later. Coming back past, she spotted a bluish mark on the back of the girl's neck.

It's the first day, and I've already managed to write-up an exceptionally bright, depressed, and physically abused student. Just great, Jada. Just great. "Please have your papers ready." She called, walking towards the first row, red pen in hand.

***

"These kids came with all the energy today." Ms. Henson, the guidance counselor sighed. She made busy heating up her Lean Cuisine in the microwave.

"Whew, honey, you sho' know what to say!" Mrs. Inglewood, the computer teacher, exclaimed. "Girl, I asked Barronnique what was the best gift she got for Christmas, and do you know what she said?"

Ms. Henson leaned in towards her, "Chiiiile, what she say? I can only imagine with that one."

"She said, I got my son." Mrs. Inglewood threw her a sideways smirk. "You know what that means," she shook her head.

"Tell me she ain't pregnant!" The counselor gasped. The microwave beeped signaling that her meal was ready.

"If I told you that, I'd be lying."

"I hate that, and I saw her this morning," she pulled the tray from the microwave. "She didn't say a thing to me. These girls are just hot, hot for any Tom, Dick, or Harry. And you can take the last two however you'd like to."

Jada sat quietly at the table, wondering if she would meet the student they discussed. Considering all that she'd heard about the teacher's lounge, the room exceeded her expectations. The cabinets were painted a cheery light blue, and all of the appliances were black and shiny. They'd nodded in her direction when she'd entered, but they flowed from topic to topic, person to person as they took turns using the bathroom.

"You know, I heard that girl might be pregnant by a grown man," Mrs. Inglewood whispered.

Jada took this as the perfect opportunity to heat up her leftovers from last night's dinner. Her ears pricked as the two women continued to gossip.

"Say it aint so!" hissed Ms. Henson "How am I the counselor, and I don't know any of this?"

"I don't know, but somebody said it's probably one of the teachers." Mrs. Inglewood whispered. "I was told it was--" She glanced in Jada's direction. "Girl, let's not influence the new girl. I'll call you later." She grabbed her lunch bag, cellphone, and keys and flounced out of the teacher's lounge, a smirk on her face.

"Look," the counselor started, crossing her arms over her chest and staring at Jada. "I hope we haven't influenced your view of the school or anything. You just gotta watch these kids, especially these girls. They'll steal your own husband if you let them. Are you married?" She flopped down in the chair next to Jada and began slurping the spaghetti between her pale lips.

"No, not yet." Jada replied. She noticed the way that her long, brown eyebrows arched at her response. She was a short woman with a small waist, but chubby legs. Her red hair almost overpowered her pale, brown skin, but it betrayed her age, making her look much younger than Jada knew to be true.

"Me either," she drawled, wiping tomato sauce from her chin. "I used to be much bigger, but then I lost all my weight because I have Lupus. Between my daughter and my job, I don't have that much time to even date. And on top of that I'm still a big chick. It's hard to get and keep a man when you big." She gazed off in deep thought.

"Well, I figured it would all come in due time." Jada exhaled. "But, ummm, I'm not rushing it. But do you like working here?"

"Are you dating someone seriously now?" She looked genuinely interested in Jada's answer.

"No, not really." She gazed at her phone. Nothing.

"Oh, okay, If you were, I was about to ask where you found him. All the good black men are either married or dead, and I've had my experience with both of 'em." She stared back at Jada, with a defeated grimace.

"I believe there's someone for everyone, regardless of size and all that. The last time I had trouble getting a date was in high school." She flipped her hair over her shoulder, her lips sliding into a small smirk. "Confidence attracts; just give it time."

Standing, Ms. Henson said, "Yeah, sometimes, you have to get 'em however you can, you know?" She threw the empty Lean Cuisine box in the garbage can and began walking towards the door. "Oh and thanks. It's good to have you here with us. Let me know if you need me." She gave a half smile before disappearing around the corner.

Jada took a long swig from her water bottle, feeling dejected and robbed. She couldn't help but feel that she'd just been forced to be a therapist, and her first session had placed a load on her shoulders. *Two more classes, and I'm done.* Her first period class had been a lesson within itself, but her second through fifth period classes had taught her lessons she wasn't sure she could describe or categorize. Her head felt like it was ready to burst from the incessant chatter of excited ninth graders and the overwhelming feeling to keep an eye on each one of them at all times. She'd been standing all day, and she was currently trying to decide whether to spend the last few minutes urinating or eating her lunch. She thought about Ms. Patel, the Algebra teacher and her hall mate, who she learned had been teaching for the past seven years and didn't seem to break a sweat. *I don't know how she does it.* She groaned aloud, leaning her head back, staring blankly at the ceiling, and ignoring the beeping of the microwave. Three o'clock could not come fast enough.

Chapter Six

Oh no, oh no, oh no. Where'd it go? Jada stood in her desk chair, swiveling from side to side, the broom in one hand and her phone in the other. She'd seen the mouse when it had entered her classroom, scurrying under the bookshelf adjacent to the door. She'd been standing in the chair since, waiting for one of the custodians to come and remove the rodent.

Mr. Oliver rounded the corner, his long and stocky frame dominating the room. "What you got in here, child?" His tiny mustache seemed to lie over his brown lips.

Jada heaved a sigh of relief. "It's under the bookcase, Mr. Oliver. A mouse---"

"That's what all this racket is about?" He stared at her with a slight grin. "You ain't neva seen no mice befo'? They gets 'em all the time." He jerked his thumb toward the door. "You eva been to dat dere gym down the hall?"

Jada shook her head.

"Awe, well, girlie, you missing a sho' nuff treat. They all up unda the bleachers." He began shuffling the books around on the book case. "See if he up in here." He peeked between books. "Must be unda the case."

"Yeah, I saw him run under it. He hasn't come out."

"You must not be from down here." He pulled one side of the bookcase out from the wall. "I'm 68 years old, and I've been here all my life. Raised my own here. Now, I'm workin' here. I used to trap mice as a boy."

"That's quite a while to be in one place, Mr. Oliver." She peeked to see if anything came out. Nothing.

"Well, you know, back in my day, we wanted to settle. Nowadays, folks don't wanna settle. They just bump with anything that help them get they rocks off." He looked back at her. "I'm not trying to be fresh with you or nuthin'. I'm just statin' facts." He pulled the other side from the wall. Nothing.

"Oh, no, sir, you're fine. I understand what you mean." Jada eased down from the chair. *Maybe I'm sleepy*, she thought.

"I sho' hope so." He walked over and eased the broom out of her hand. "But like I was saying, young folks just want everythang fast now. Sex, babies, money, houses, cars. It just don't make no sense. Being grown ain't all it's cracked up to be." He began sweeping the broom under the left side of the bookcase.

Jada drifted into thoughts of recent conversations with her mom and Caleb. Her mom had been encouraging her to slow down and enjoy her life. "It's not all about work," she'd said. Caleb had been saying the same, but, ironically, as she'd heard them, they hadn't sounded the same.

"And ungrateful, too." Mr. Oliver continued. "Folks so ungrateful nowadays. Like at this here school, I'm the custodian, right?" He looked back at Jada.

She nodded her head. "That you are, Mr. Oliver."

"You right I am." He continued swiping the broom. "But what I ain't is a maid. You know half these teachers won't empty they own trash? They see it full, running over with trash and leave it like that for me. Gum and open juice bottles everywhere. That's how I knew you were the real deal. Come here some days, and you already done emptied the trash. I ain't seen kids leave no chip bags or empty bottles all on your flo'. The desk still be in straight rows. That's how you know if a teacher gon' make it here or not." He swiped the broom from left to right under the bookcase.

The small brown mouse ran from under the case, towards the door.

"There it is!" Jada squealed. She jumped back onto the chair.

"Ahh, I got it." He took two giant steps and brought the broom down hard on the little rodent. It lay on its back, feet in the air, wriggling. The broom came down once more, and it moved no more. "See, you gotta be patient. That's the only way you gone get somewhere." He scooped it into the dustpan. "I'll bring your pan back in a little while after I clean it."

Jada climbed from the chair, careful not to get too close to the curled up rodent. "Thanks so much, Mr. Oliver. If no one else says it, just know that I, for one, appreciate you, especially after today." She laughed.

He chuckled, dumped the rodent in the trash bag, and pulled the bag out of the can. "Means a lot. You gotta stop running from these little fellas. They're not even as big as that eraser over there." He tied the bag tightly.

"I know, I know." She nodded her head slowly. "They just move so fast."

"Well, you see now that even thangs moving fast meet trouble after while." He tipped the bib of his baseball hat in her direction before turning the corner."

She nodded thoughtfully and began reorganizing the book shelves, wondering if asking Caleb to speed up their relationship had done more harm than good.

***

Jada watched the new student shuffle into the class. It had only taken her the first week to learn all of the students' names, so they were now scattered about the room.

"Hi, what's your name?" she asked as she approached the girl.

The girl's dark skin glowed under the fluorescent light, dark circles from what Jada perceived to be lack of sleep engulfed her big, sad eyes. Her lips seemed to be in a natural pout.

"It's Demetria," the girl answered absentmindedly.

So, this is mystery girl, she thought, marking her present in her gradebook. "It's really nice to have you here with us." She smiled at the girl. "Here's the syllabus for the class; we'll schedule a time to talk so that we can get you caught up, okay?"

Demetria looked up at the ceiling and sighed loudly before plopping into an empty desk.

"Okay, ladies and gentlemen, today we're going to read a very short story by Gary Soto called "The Talk." It's about two teenage boys, who find themselves very unattractive. Have any of you ever felt like that?" She glanced from row to row.

The students looked at her, some glancing back and forward at each other but remaining silent. She realized the complexity of her question. It would require them to open up about a sensitive part of themselves, but that's what she wanted.

"Okay, so I'll start," she said. "I grew up thinking that I was very unattractive. I think you guys call it being hurt, right? Wait. No, ya'll call it the struggle!" She clapped her hands together and beamed with accomplishment, her eyes peering back at the students for verification. The students began to chuckle and murmur to each other.

"Ms. Harris, where you learn dat at?" Ashton laughed. He'd easily become the class joker but also a gem in Jada's eyes, always the source of laughter and energy that every teacher needs in a first period class. Yet, she had learned that he was one of the most suspended students in the school. He puzzled her in so many ways.

Jada grinned. "After being around ya'll for so long, it rubs off." The class chuckled. "Like I was saying, you guys, growing up, I was picked on for being darker skinned and chubby. On top of that, I wore glasses, and I had braces."

"Oooohh, the struggle was real forreal," One student, Luiz, yelled from the back corner of the room.

"Ms. Harris had that hurt!" Clinton yelled. The class roared with laughter.

Jada couldn't help but giggle. "Yes, yes, I did. It was bad. I felt awful every day. There were times that the school bully, her name was Mercedes---"

"Ole girl was named after the car?" Ashton asked, his eyebrows wriggled with humor.

"Yes, she was." Her response was followed by more thunderous laughter. "Anyway, she found something negative to say about me every day. And then, I had this crush named Octavious. Oh, he was the cutest boy in school, I thought. But, he would make fun of me by walking up to me and saying, 'Hey, my friend wanna talk to you' only for the friend to yell out, 'I don't want that fat, black girl.' And they would all laugh. It was one big joke, and I actually believed I was those things."

The room was silent.

Ashton broke the silence. "Why you let them do you like that? I woulda checked they as--"

"Ashton!" Jada snapped. "Watch it!"

"My fault, Ms. Harris." He scooted down in the desk. "You should've checked they a---butts---- back. You was weak for that one."

"Oh, yes, I was." She began to walk around the room. "My self-esteem was so low that even when my mama bought me this baaad leather pantsuit in 6th grade, I told her I didn't like it because I knew everyone would make fun of me. But I really did like it."

Jada noticed the tears in Demetria's dark eyes. She had latched onto every word, and Jada wasn't sure why.

"So, I'll ask again. Any of you felt that way?" A round of hands flew up in the air. "Okay, Keisha, do you mind sharing your experience?"

The girl sunk timidly into her desk. "Well," she spoke softly. "A lot of people make fun of you if you don't have the right shoes or if your hair ain't a certain length or sum'" She looked down at the desk.

"Thanks for sharing, Keisha." The girl nodded. "Any of you been made fun of because of your clothes, hair, or size?"

Everyone raised their hands except for Ashton, Luiz, and Vanessa. Since referring Vanessa and speaking with the counselor about the marks on her arm, Jada hadn't heard much from her. She spoke only when spoken to; it unnerved Jada that she still hadn't broken down the wall. She couldn't help but feel at fault because of their first encounter. She made a mental note to speak to Coach Young about her.

"Okay, so now you all know that you are not alone. Grab the textbook under your desk and turn to "The Talk.""

"What page that on?" One student blurted out.

"Guys, use the table of contents." She began passing out the vocabulary worksheets for the story.

"She stay sayin' that." Ashton said, roughly turning the pages.

Jada smiled at herself, glimpsing Vanessa and Demetria's somber faces out of the corner of her eye.

***

Coach Young leaned against the black-stained, steel desk, crossing his ankles. His checkered orange and brown socks peeked from under his beige slacks. He crossed his arms over his chest and smiled slyly at Jada. His eyes lowered to hazel brown slicks as he slowly dragged his tongue across his dark, smoker's lips.

"Sooo," he drawled. "The infamous Ms. Harris finally darkens my door." He stroked his budding beard. "To what do I owe the honor?" He pushed off the desk.

Jada took a step back. "Well, I came to speak with you about Vanessa."

He seemed to sober immediately. "Umm, what's going on with her?"

"It's been a few weeks, and I still can't break down the wall with her. She's so detached in class." She eased into one of the larger desks. "Coach Lewis suggested that I speak with you since you work closely with her."

"Ah-um-well, yeah." he scrunched up his pants and settled behind the desk. "Vanessa is--well, how can I say this?" He nibbled on a pen top. "She's had a rough childhood. Her mom's young, in and out of jail----father in jail for molesting Vanessa and her older sister."

Jada winced at the matter-of-fact tone with which he spoke.

"It's tough for some of these kids, you know?"

She searched his face for sincerity. "Yeah, I see that. So how did you do it?"

"Do what?" He leaned forward and rested his chin on his linked fingers.

"Get close to her." She maneuvered uncomfortably under his steady gaze.

His lips spread into a sideways grin. She felt that he sensed her discomfort.

"It's hard to say, but I had to get her to trust me first. So, in the beginning, I checked on her often. I shared sensitive parts of my own life with her, you know?" She nodded. "When she scored well on an assignment, I gave her candy and a card or brought her lunch. Next thing you know," he rubbed his hands together, then clapped. "She was opening up to me in so many ways. Eventually, she began to trust and respect me."

"Wow. I didn't know you had that in you, Coach Young." she scoffed, standing.

He spread his large, caramel-toned hand across his chest in mock injury. "Why, Ms. Harris! I would hate to think that I'd made a negative first impression." He pouted, pretending to wipe away tears.

"See, it's hard for me to take you serious." She shook her head, chuckling softly. "I usually see you standing back from everything. You know, not getting too involved with all the school stuff and the students."

"So, in other words, you think I show up just for the check." He stood, shoving his hands in his pockets, his head slightly tilted and his eyes fixated on her intensely.

"Well, n--umm. Yes." She linked her fingers in front of her black and white striped torso. "Like I said, you walk around like you're all smooth and stuff, like nothing else really matters; so, I just---" Her words trailed off.

"It's cool. I get it." He took a few steps toward her. "But, I heard you say that you think I'm smooth." He stepped closer.

Jada fumbled to scoop the folders off the desk. "No, I said that you *think* you're smooth. I'm not that easily impressed, Coach Young." She stepped backwards.

He grinned, pulling on his chin hair. "What exactly do I have to do to impress you?" He inched forward, their chests not far from each other. "Because I think you'll find that we have a lot in common." He twirled her gray scarf around his finger.

She pulled the scarf out of his grasp. "I'm not looking to find out." She turned and marched towards the door.

"All females play that game!" He called. She turned to look at him. "I'll break down those walls, Ms. Harris. All of them!" He winked at her before strolling back to his desk, whistling.

Jada reflected on his words as she walked back to her class. Being in the presence of Coach Young always unsettled her in ways she couldn't describe. His arrogance irritated her. His eyes always appeared to be expecting something, illuminating with anticipation. His grin was that of an alley rat, crouching behind a garbage dumpster at the close of a city diner. It bothered her even more that she'd initially found him attractive, but now, she couldn't shake the feeling that she needed to brush her teeth and take a fresh bath. She peeked at her watch, only thirty minutes left in her planning period. She dipped into the girl's bathroom to wash her hands and primp her hair.

The sounds of muffled sobs halted her hands. She rounded the corner and peeked under the stalls. A familiar pair of purple sequin booties shuffled under the last stall.

"Vanessa?" Jada tapped on the door. "This is Ms. Harris. Are you okay?"

"I'm fine." The girl choked out. "Please leave me alone."

"Now, Vanessa, you know I can't do that. Will you please come out?"

"No. I said I'm fine."

"Well, you know people don't usually cry in a bathroom when they're fine." Jada leaned against the door.

"I do." The girl replied, rattling toilet paper off the dispenser. The bathroom echoed as she blew hard into the paper.

"Okay, tell me what you're happy about then."

Silence. She thought of Coach Young's words, *Get her to trust you.*

"You know, this is familiar to me." Jada sighed. "Being in a bathroom stall crying. One time I cried in the bathroom during recess because no one picked me to be on their team for Red Rover. Oh, my little 9 year-old feelings were so hurt. I stayed in the bathroom for the whole recess. Then, in high school, I cried because I liked this guy named Marcus Meer, and no matter how much I dressed up, curled my hair, or slathered my lips with gloss, he just didn't see me. That day, he'd asked me to hook him up with one of my classmates, Tina. She was light-skinned, petite, and she talked real fast, used all of the hood lingo, and he was a tall, lanky basketball player that wore glasses. In my 9th grade mind, they all wanted girls like her. So, I cried for a minute or two in the bathroom wondering, *what's so wrong with me?*" She side-eyed the stall. The girl's sobbing had turned to small sniffles. "Vanessa, are you there?"

Her question was met with silence.

"If you need to talk, I'm always willing to listen. You just listened to me, so it would only be fair for me to return the favor." She knocked softly on the door.

"Did you do it?" The girl asked clearing her throat.

"Do what?"

"D-did you hook them up?"

Jada smiled at herself. "I did actually. I felt so foolish afterwards. I didn't expect Tina, my friend, to go for it. Oh, but girl, she did. I was so mad." She chuckled inwardly.

The door latch clicked loudly. "Yeah, that wasn't a smart move." The girl muffled, peeking from behind the door.

Jada pushed off the wall. "Hey. At my age then, well, your age now, bad decisions are expected. Are you okay?"

The girl slowly shook her head. "I started bleeding."

Jada looked the scrawny girl up and down. "What do you mean? Are you hurt? Where's the blood coming from?"

"I-I don't know. It's only in my panties, and my stomach hurts real bad." She gazed at the floor. "I tried to call my mom, but she said she was at work and hung up."

Jada felt her anxiety ease. It was replaced with sadness when she noted the worry lines in the girl's forehead and the frightened look in her eyes. "Vanessa, it sounds like you got your menstrual cycle." The girl looked confused. "It can also be called a period. All girls go through it once every month, even me." She rubbed the girl's arm. "It's nothing to be ashamed of or scared about. It just means that you've made the first step towards becoming a woman."

"A-a woman?" The first glimmer of excitement seemed to fly across the girl's face, disappearing as quickly as it had appeared.

"Yep. Welcome." She stuck out her hand.

The girl slowly reached for her hand and shook it softly.

"Now, I'm going to take you to the teacher's lounge so that you can have some privacy; while you're in there take off your bottoms, get some paper towels and wash yourself off. There might be a lot of blood but just use a little soap and water to wipe yourself as clean as possible, okay?"

"What am I gonna do about my underwear and pants? I can't go back to class with these." She tugged at her navy blue pants.

"I'm going to run to the store, get you some underwear and pants, and some pads. Do you know what pads are?"

The girl shook her head. Jada had to keep herself from frowning.

"Okay," Jada took off her suit jacket and wrapped it around the girl. "Let's go to the teachers' lounge. You wash up and just wait for me, okay?"

The girl nodded. They walked quickly to the teacher's lounge. Jada yanked extra towels from the dispenser and ushered the girl into the single stall. "Do you remember what I said?" The girl nodded. "Good. Now, lock the door. I'll be back."

The pinballs in Jada's minds were bouncing from corner to corner. She nearly ran to her classroom to retrieve a pad from her rolling bag. She jogged out the door, slamming into Mr. Jackson's purple and green plaid chest. He caught her by her arms.

"Whoa! What's going on, Ms. Harris?" He frowned in concern.

"I-I, well, V-. One of the girls has a woman issue right now, so I'm trying to get her situated before the bell rings."

He crossed his arms over his chest. "Do you need anything?"

"Yes, she needs a new pair of pants."

"Did you call home?"

"I didn't, but she said she talked to her mom, who told her she was busy at work."

"Wow," he sighed loudly, shaking his glasses-framed head. "Let me try to call her. I'm sure we have some pants in the lost and found." They walked briskly towards the office.

"Mr. Jackson, she's already embarrassed enough. I don't think giving her some pants from the lost and found is a good idea." She stopped him mid stride, lightly grabbing his arm.

"What other option do we have?"

"I can run up the street really quickly and buy her a pair."

"You won't make it back in time for class. I'll have Coach Young do it." He pulled his cell phone from his back pocket.

"No!" She hissed. "This is not a man's problem. It will only make her feel more uncomfortable. I told her *I* would be back. The longer we stand here, the less time I have."

"Okay, okay." He closed his phone and slipped it back into his pocket. "I'll delay the bell by a few minutes."

Jada yelled her thanks and pulled her kitten heels off as she jogged to the parking lot.

***

Vanessa seemed to tiptoe out of the bathroom, her sockless feet slapping against the tile. Jada examined the snug fit of the navy blue cargo pants on her slim legs. She had guessed that she could fit the same size as her younger sister, and Jada was surprised that she'd been correct. The girl's walk was stiff, and her eyes seemed to ask, *Is this normal?*

"It's normal to feel like you want to ball up," she assured her. "You're probably going to feel like that for the next three or four days."

The girl nodded. "W-w-will I need more pads?"

"For sure. Now-" She handed her a slip of paper. "On that paper is all that you need to know about taking care of yourself for the next few days. I bought you two packs of pads. You should keep at least two pads in your book bag everyday so that while you're at school, you can change them."

"Will everyone else know that I got my period?"

Jada chuckled. "No, ma'am. Not unless you tell them. But you shouldn't tell anyone about it except your mom, or a very, very close relative."

"My mom won't care." She cast her eyes to the floor, sliding her feet back and forth across the tile.

"What about your dad?"

"He's in jail."

"Oh, well, you can talk to me." She placed her hand on the girls arm. "I'll give you my number, and you just call or text if you have any questions. Okay?"

The girl nodded. She looked up suddenly. "What about my boyfriend? Can we still---?" Her words trailed off, and she peeked at Jada through long eyelashes.

Jada couldn't help but feel uncomfortable. "Ummm, I can't say much on that other than no, you shouldn't do *that*." The beeping of the microwave interrupted the awkward silence. Jada seized the opportunity to change the subject and stopped the beeping. "Umm, put your socks on, and I made you some hot chocolate. It'll ease some of the pain you're feeling."

The bell sounded to change classes.

"Once you're ready, just go to Mrs. Inglewood's class. I'll let her know you're coming." She walked towards the door.

"Ms. Harris," Vanessa called. Jada stopped, her hand on the door knob. "Thanks."

Jada smiled at the girl before quietly closing the door. *My advisor was wrong*, she thought. *Gossiping isn't the only thing that happens in the teacher's lounge.* She couldn't wait to tell Caleb.

Chapter Seven

"Are you even listening to me?" She eased her gold, PT Cruiser onto the highway. A wreck up ahead caused traffic to move at a snail's pace. Next to her, a maroon Mustang blared Tupac, the volume of the car's bass causing Jada's steering wheel to vibrate under her fingers. She was clearly irritated, and Caleb wasn't making it better.

"I heard you, Jada." He groaned into the phone.

"Okay, what did I say then?"

"You were fussing about not really having talked to me."

"Fussing? Is that what we're calling it now?" She stared at the phone. "I didn't know that girlfriends being worried about their boyfriends was called fussing."

"I didn't know a girlfriend just walked away from her man either." He hissed into the phone.

"Wow, are you really saying that again? We've talked about this so many times. I'm seriously tired of it."

"No, *you* talked about it! I never had a say!" He sounded helpless and annoyed. "You never said, 'Babe, what about *we* do this or *we* do that. Everything was *Jada* is doing this and *Jada* is doing that. You never factored me into your plans, so why now, do you wanna act surprised?"

Jada *was* surprised. The truth in his words stung, and tears gathered in the corners of her eyes. She *hadn't* asked for him to weigh-in on her decision throughout the entire process. She'd simply brought up things over dinner, but he had never offered any feedback, which had irked her in so many ways. Now, she realized that while she'd been wanting him to be more assertive, he had been wanting her to be more vulnerable, asking for his input. But it bothered her that even now she didn't feel guilty about not having included him. Three years and he still didn't bring anything but love to the table. She'd been battling within herself constantly. *Was love enough?* She couldn't help but hear her mother saying, "Love does not pay bills." Tears began to flow, as she thought of their relationship, if that was what you could even call it now.

"Caleb?" She spoke softly.

"Yeah?" His voice sounded strained. She couldn't help but wonder if he had been crying too.

"You're right. I didn't think of you. For that, I'm sorry." She waited patiently for his reply.

"I-it's okay. I know why you didn't." He sighed into the phone. "Don't you think I wanna have the job and security that I know you need? I'm trying, man."

Jada cradled the phone with her hand, easing into an opening in the free-flowing next lane. "I know. I just couldn't bank on potential, and right now, that's all you bring to the table."

"But I love you, man. Tell me you don't trust me. You can't. Tell me I don't respect you as my woman. Tell me I don't show you love often, shower you with kisses, hugs, and gifts on special days. Like, when I have the money, I take you out. I try my best to spoil you the best that I can. Can you tell me I don't do any of that?" His voice cracked.

"No," she whispered. "I can't tell you that."

"So, are you really about to sit on this phone and say all that don't mean nothing if I don't have the perfect job?"

"I never said you needed the perfect job. You could be a doggone sanitation worker, and I would feel better, but right now, you're working odd jobs, and you haven't done anything to protect your, well, our future. Like, you want me to sit around and be okay with it, but you know me. I'm ambitious. I'll be forging ahead, paying majority of the bills, and you'll be satisfied getting by."

"No, Jada, I keep you grounded."

"I don't want a man to keep me *grounded*! I want him to soar with me." She pressed the gas, weaving between cars headed north.

"But you want it on *your* time!" He yelled into the phone.

"The past three years have been *your* time!" She shouted back. "For three whole years, I've been telling you to do something, anything, so that *this*--this right here--this whole conversation, could be avoided! Tell me I'm lying!"

He spoke softly, in defeat. "Man, you know---" He sighed. "Do you remember that mountain I drew a while back? When I would say, 'it might be bigger than you; it might be bigger than me, but it will never be bigger than you and me.'" I meant that, but apparently there is a mountain bigger than us."

"Caleb--" Her voice cracked.

"It's all good. I gotta go."

"But--we haven't---"

"Just don't move on on me. Give me time to show you."

“O-okay.”

“I’ll talk to you later.” The line went silent.

Jada dropped the phone in the passenger seat and gripped the steering wheel tighter with both hands. She released a loud scream as tears fell to her lap. Her phone lit up with an unknown number, but she ignored its ringing, sending the caller to voicemail. She drove faster and faster with no destination in mind. She couldn’t shake the solemn feeling of loneliness. Even though she hadn’t spoken to Caleb often over the past few weeks, she knew that this time would be different. Essentially, she was single again. She hadn’t wanted *this*, this abrupt end to them, to the connection they’d made over Philly Cheesesteaks and chocolate chip cookies, or s’mores over the fireplace, nights where action movies put her to sleep on his hairy chest, to times when he bristled under her playful complaints about his mother’s cooking. She shook her head violently, wishing the memories away but to no avail. She jumped out of her daze when her phone buzzed loudly. She snatched it from the seat.

“Hello,” she croaked.

“Hoooney,” the squeaky, male voice shouted. “You sound exactly how I did after my first month of teaching.”

“Ummm, who is this?” She pressed the phone closer to her ear, becoming instantly alert and anxious.

"It's Mr. Williams from school. You know, the Social Studies teacher."

"Oh, sorry." She swallowed. "How'd you get my number?"

"Girl, I have everyone's number. Told you that you family now!" He spoke in a terrible country accent, giggling. "But look, some of us usually meet up for dinner every now and then, so I'm calling to invite you. We're going to Feluccio's on Grand and Avion in Millhaven. You should come!"

Jada grimaced at the idea of pulling herself together and being in anyone's company right now. She wasn't feeling very festive. Yet, maybe that's what she needed to get her mind off Caleb. "You know what, I'll meet you there."

"Oh my gosh, how great!" He yipped in her ear, causing her to hold the phone a few inches from her face. "We'll see you in about twenty minutes, Hon."

"Okay." Jada clicked off the line and merged into the right lane, turning on her turning signal to exit the highway. *This is exactly what I need right now*, she thought, dialing her mother.

***

"Then, he came in smelling like pure sh--"

"Mrs. Calloway!" Mr. Vincent, the school's new art teacher, interrupted her. Sitting across from Jada, he overlapped his hands on top of the table, a small smirk highlighting his chubby, brown-skin face. His eyelids were like hoods over his brown eyes, as he laughed boisterously. "You said he smelled like what?" Her knowing glance sent him and the others into another fit of laughter.

"You know exactly what he smelled like. What he always smell like. Family should be ashamed." She sipped from her straw exaggeratedly. Her table mates roared in amusement.

Jada forced a lopsided smile. She didn't hear the facilitator's comment in the same way that everyone else had. Mr. Williams was holding his tiny pudge of a stomach; Mr. Vincent was constantly wiping tears from his eyes. Ms. Henson, the school counselor, chuckled while staring at her phone, and Mr. Harper, the economics teacher laughed between bites of fries.

"Calloway, tell us why he smell like that, child," Mr. Vincent urged, leaning forward and resting his chin on his hand.

"You asking the wrong person. Ms. Henson is the counselor." She flicked her wrist towards the counselor, biting into her meatball and marinara sandwich.

Ms. Henson placed her phone face down on the table. "I was told that his family has trouble keeping the lights and stuff on in the house, so they take baths every few days." She cut into her lemon-seasoned chicken nonchalantly. "I don't know."

"Every few days?" Calloway questioned, her eyebrows raised. "Try every year. These students lie. I don't think Steven has ever really taken baths. He been smelling foul since he got in the 9th grade." She stabbed a fry and popped it in her mouth. "Ms. Harris, you teach him, right?" She stared at Jada expectantly.

"I do, but I don't like to speak on stuff like that. You never know what might be going on with a student." She shifted uncomfortably under their intense gazes.

Mr. Williams and Ms. Calloway exchanged glances.

"I know what ain't going on!" Ms. Calloway leaned forward, taking time to look about the table. "Bathing!" She pointed towards the ceiling. "That's what's not going on in that house!" Her laughter was deep and sinister.

Jada leaned back in her chair, wondering why she'd bothered to come. This wasn't easing her mind in the way that she'd thought it would. Most of the dinner had been spent talking about someone from the school, especially the students. She knew that teachers discussed different students, but the conversation was much different from what she was used to. Rather than discuss their attitudes or progress, the group preferred to discuss their bad weaves, poor families, or lack of intelligence. It uneased Jada to think that these were the same people that many of the students loved. There was never a time when Ms. Henson didn't have students lounging around in her office during their lunch, or when Mr. Williams had students popping in throughout the day just to say hello.

"Well, I think I'm going to call it a night." Jada reached into her jacket pocket and placed the money in the tiny envelope to cover her bill.

"You're leaving so soon?" Mr. Williams pouted, folding his arms over his chest.

"Yeah, it's close to my bedtime." She stood and pushed her chair under the table. "Thanks for inviting me. See you all tomorrow."

Mrs. Calloway leered at her over the top of her Margarita glass, as Ms. Henson tapped intensely on her phone and Mr. Vincent wriggled his fingers towards her in farewell.

"I'll walk you out," Mr. Harper rose, grabbing his jacket.

"Oh, no need." She raised her hand in protest.

"Harris, we're in Millhaven. It can be dangerous. Just let him walk you to your car." Mr. Williams peered over his black-rimmed glasses while sipping from his large Sex on the Beach.

"Okay, fine." She began walking towards the restaurant door; he followed closely behind her. "Okay, here I am." She announced, approaching her car and unlocking the door.

"Cool." He pulled the door open, waiting for her to climb in. "Look," he leaned down. "I could tell you weren't very comfortable in there. Don't take what they say too serious. It's just jokes and stuff."

"Hmm, if you say so." She reached to close the door.

He held it open. "Imma let you go, but we should do this again. You know, without the rest of them." He lowered his eyes to the ground before slowly meeting her stare.

"I don't know you." She started the engine.

"That's why we need to meet up." He grinned. "Like a date."

She glanced down at her phone. "I don't think so. I'm just getting out of a relationship--err--I think." She sighed heavily. "Clearly, I'm not ready to date yet."

"Well, okay. What if we don't call it a date?"

Jada examined his face. The lines around his eyes made him look about forty, but his purple pants and beige polo shirt *did* make him appear younger. His lips slowly moved into a lopsided smile that revealed sparkling white teeth, shaped by a well-groomed goatee. He looked different from other men she'd dated. Maybe I *could* eventually be attracted to him, she thought.

"We'll see."

He seemed satisfied with her answer. "Works for me. Have a good night, Jada." He pushed her door closed.

She fastened her seatbelt, watching his big and tall form saunter into the restaurant. She'd never dated a man bigger than her or that much older than her before. That would definitely be a change. She shifted her car into gear and zoomed out of the restaurant parking lot.

Chapter *Eight*

Jada fumbled towards the resounding alarm that read 5:15 A.M. Flipping onto her stomach, she reached to the other side of the bed, just barely tapping the off button. Her cat, Duchess, took the opportunity to climb onto her back, purring softly.

"Duch," she groaned. "It's too early, girl." She slowly turned on her side, and the cat slid onto the mattress, meowing in protest. "Now, you're mad at me." She threw her chubby legs over the side of the bed, wriggled her feet into her slippers, gathered the grey and black cat into her arms, and shuffled into the living room. Since she'd started teaching, she had made it her goal to buy at least two of her dream furniture pieces with every paycheck. So far, she'd purchased a zebra print chaise, a turquoise tapestry rug, and a leather sectional. She was proud of herself for sticking with her commitment and budgeting enough to keep her afloat. Duchess began to shift in her arms. "Okay, let's get you fed." She scratched the cat's underbelly; she purred with satisfaction.

At the sound of the chicken and liver can being opened, the cat fought to be free. Jada lowered her to the ground and poured water into her tiny bowl, taking a few minutes to watch her eat. After every bite, Duchess stared back at her, expectantly. She rubbed her gently and strolled into the bathroom. She only had thirty minutes to get dressed.

Jada curled the last strand of hair into a tight curl that fell on the side of her forehead. She feathered and teased it while twisting and turning in the mirror. Her cat jumped onto the bathroom counter.

"What do you think, Duch? Yay or nay?" The cat meowed while claiming her spot in the corner. Jada examined the new auburn highlights she'd put in her hair on a whim last night, and she had to admit that her hair looked far more funky and eccentric than she would normally wear it, but she liked it. It was bold, fresh, and youthful; it was a new her. She hadn't worn her hair down to school, so she knew the students' tongues would wag when they saw her, but she didn't mind. In the last week, she'd learned that sometimes students like Vanessa came to school just to see what clothes or up-do she had. Since then, she'd taken great pains when considering her wardrobe. If it would motivate more students to come, she didn't mind putting in the extra effort; plus, she needed a style update anyway to accommodate her new career and freedom.

Walking out of the door with her white, long-sleeved collar shirt under a knee-length and red, hip-hugging dress and her hair framing her face in soft waves, she hadn't felt this free in years.

***

Jada stifled a yawn as she pulled into her usual parking space. Newfound freedom, clearly, came with a price tag. The restless nights of tossing and turning, awaking in the middle of the night to check her phone for any messages were taking a toll. She found herself going back and forth in her head but ultimately deciding she had made the right decision.

She thought of how she normally plastered on a smile whenever she stood before students, unwilling to show them how exhausted she really was. That's what she thought made teachers actors and actresses. Regardless of her problems, she never allowed the students to see it. She practiced her smile in the rearview mirror while primping her hair, but paused when she spotted Mrs. Kimble, the Chemistry teacher, hurrying from the fieldhouse.

Mrs. Kimble fumbled with the buttons on her shirt as she approached her black Tahoe. She opened the passenger side door and pulled out her blue and red backpack, slipped on a pair of nude stilettos, and reapplied her lipstick while looking in the side view mirror.

Jada turned to get a better view of her and watched her as she ran her fingers through her shoulder-length hair before swiping her thumb across her darkened lower lash line, removing the smeared eyeliner and mascara from her brown skin. Content with her appearance, she folded her pea coat in the crook of her arm and sashayed into the building, her heels clicking with each step.

Jada looked back at the field house, wondering who would come out next. It was clear that Mrs. Kimble was having an affair. *But with who?* She thought. Just then, the school bell rang, which indicated that it was time for all teachers to be in their classrooms. Jada groaned and snatched up her work bag, jogged up the sidewalk and yanked open the door. She slammed into a soft and petite frame.

"Whoa." Mrs. Kimble's raspy voice explained. She held both hands up to lessen the impact. "It's just the tardy bell, Ms. Harris. They won't penalize you."

Flustered, Jada exhaled. "Great. Sorry." She bent to retrieve the scarf that had fallen to the floor as a result of their collision.

"I saw your car. I thought you were already inside." Mrs. Kimble stared into her eyes.

"Oh, no. I, umm, well, I just really got here. Sat in the car for a minute."

"Oh,--" her eyes widened. "Oh, my. I'm so embarrassed. Y-you probably saw me coming from the field house." The woman's eyes darted down the hall and back to Jada.

Jada remained silent.

"You're not married are you?"

Jada shook her head. "No, I'm not."

"Good." She noticed the confused look on Jada's face. "No, wait-" she touched her arm. "I'm not trying to discourage you from getting married. I'm just saying that for some reason when you get married, you lose that spark, that sense of adventure that you had as two love-struck bunnies dating. You get comfortable. So, my husband and I are trying to put that spark back in our marriage." She nudged Jada with her elbow. "If you know what I mean."

Jada shifted her weight to one leg. "Oh, um, okay. But why the fieldhouse?" She asked out of curiosity.

"W-well, my husband, Andre, used to play football in high school. T-that's how we met in high school. He was the jock, the star player, and I was new on the cheerleading team. He asked me out, and we were inseparable after that. He was my first *everything*; first date, first kiss, first--" she stopped abruptly and cleared her throat. "You get it. But yeah, we're trying to revisit those times."

"Umm, okay." Jada began walking toward her classroom on the adjoining hall. "See you later."

"I trust that this will stay between us ladies, Ms. Harris." She called.

"Who am I going to tell? But you might want to be more careful." Jada gave a slight wave before turning back up the hall.

She was far more awake now than she had been upon her arrival. She thought of Caleb and all their talks of marriage. She hadn't thought of how their attraction for one another might fizzle. Her imagination had always been full of thought-provoking conversations, followed by long nights of passion. Now, Mrs. Kimble made her wonder otherwise. *But never the fieldhouse*, she thought.

The bell rang for students to enter the building. She groaned loudly, quickly inserting her key in the door and hustling into the cold classroom. She started her desktop computer, pulled her lesson plan book from her bag, and wrote the day's objective on the front board. The monitor dinged, alerting her to new emails. She hastened back to her desk and opened an email from Mr. Jackson. Vanessa's mother wanted to meet with her during her planning period. Jada rolled her eyes toward the ceiling and set out to greet her students as they strolled into the classroom.

***

"I don't need Ms. Bougie over here doing anything for *my* child!" Vanessa's mother sat across from Jada and Mr. Jackson at the wooden, mahogany-stained conference table. Her hair was covered in a leopard print bonnet, and her petite frame was clad in a low-cut purple shirt with sequins along her shoulders. The low neckline revealed a paw print tattoo between her cleavage and what Jada assumed to be Vanessa's name just above her heart.

"There's no need for name calling, Ms. Pigues." He placed his pen on the table and laced his fingers together. "What exactly is Ms. Harris doing for Vanessa that you don't like?"

"Too much. That's what she's doing." She scowled at Jada. "She buys her pads and stuff. That's my child! I can buy *my* child pads and stuff. I didn't even know she'd gotten her period until I found some new panties that I know I didn't buy. Then, Vanessa told me."

"Well, Ms. Pigues, Vanessa got her menstrual cycle at school," Jada explained. "She tried to call you, but you were at work."

"I dunno bout any of that." She stared back at Jada.

"Ms. Pigues," Mr. Jackson chimed in. "I called your job as well. Every time your colleagues transferred me to you, the phone just rang and rang. And the alternate emergency number we have for Vanessa is disconnected. So, with my approval, Ms. Harris did what we thought was best, which was to get her some new undergarments and toiletries." He leaned forward, resting both elbows on the table.

"That other number is her grandma's number, and her phone off right now. And look, I get all that, but from here on out, I don't want you doing anything for my child." She readjusted the bonnet on her head. "All I hear is Ms. Harris did this and Ms. Harris did that."

"Well, I can't make any promises. I don't want to overstep my boundaries, but if Vanessa needs something I can't say that I won't help. Isn't that what you want from teachers?"

"You gone feed ha'? What about lettin' ha' live witchu'? See, you can play this little ima-save-this-little-black-child game all you want, but I see through you. Black chicks like you come in this school acting like you better than everybody. Ya'll get to filling these kids heads up wit all this dream bullcrap, have them looking down on they own parents, but you ain't feedin' ha'. You'n know nothing bout ha', bout us, this community. You a visitor in our land," she snarled, slapping the table.

Jada was taken aback by the slicing tone of her words. They fell out of her mouth smoothly as if they'd been there for years. Sitting there, Jada didn't see a mother concerned for her child. She saw a child herself, one unhappy, miserable, and defeated in ways she couldn't imagine. Yet, a part of Jada felt guilty, as though certain parts had been indeed true.

"I can assure you," Mr. Jackson began, invading her thoughts, "that Ms. Harris has Vanessa's best interest at heart. They had a rocky start, but now, everything is okay. Vanessa's grades have improved significantly, and I know that at the end of the day, we all want what's best for her. So, we will continue to communicate with you as situations arise so that there won't be any confusion. Will that work?"

The woman snorted. "I guess. I just needed to show my face 'cause I don't want anything gettin' twisted. I'm her momma. Point, blank, and period." She shot Jada a fiery glance before pushing from the table, grabbing her car keys, and standing.

"Okay, well, I want to thank you for coming, Ms. Pigues." He and Jada stood. He shook the woman's hand.

"Yes, it was nice to meet you." Jada smiled and nodded in her direction.

"Uh huh," the woman yanked open the door and disappeared around the corner.

Mr. Jackson turned to her. "Don't let it get to you. As long as you're a teacher, you will always have those parents."

"Mr. Jackson?" The secretary stuck her head in the door. "Don't forget about your Cooking Club meeting with Mrs. Kimble."

He glanced at his watch. "Oh, right. Thanks, Ms. Allen." He gathered the stack of papers from the table. "Gotta run."

Jada sank into the plush chair, exhaling loudly. She watched as Mrs. Kimble rounded the corner. Her brown skin seemed to color when she spotted Jada, probably because of the little secret between them. She nodded towards her and continued to Mr. Jackson's office, closing the door softly behind her.

"Ms. Harris," the secretary stood in the door. "I have the workbooks and dictionaries that you ordered."

"Great!" Jada exclaimed, jumping from the seat. She couldn't have asked for better news to brighten an already dismal day.

***

"Okay, ladies and gentlemen, let's talk about drama." She looked at each one of the students in her fifth period class. "Tell me what you know about drama."

Denise, a hazel-toned girl with taupe faux locks raised her hand. "Drama is when there's a whole buncha pettiness going on, people fighting and arguing and stuff."

Jada grimaced at the girl spitting out the words as if they were venomous. "Okay, we have Denise's answer. Who else?"

Chris shoved his hand in the air. "It's when things don't go as planned. You know, like what we talked about before---umm" He looked over at his friend for help. The boy shrugged his shoulders in response. "Oh, yeah! Situational irony!" He snapped his finger, excitedly. "Like, I can see that causing drama when things don't go as planned."

"Oh, wow. Good job using some of our past vocabulary, Chris." Jada beamed. "And you're right; I can see that causing some drama. Anyone else?" She scanned the room.

"It can be what some of us go through every day. Parents never getting along, or even losing a parent." another girl spoke solemnly, a downcast gleam in her eyes. She leaned back in her seat, as if to signal that she was done talking for today.

Jada wanted to hear more. She looked down at the lesson plan notes for the day, which indicated that at this time, she should've been handing out notes on drama, but she couldn't shake the feeling that the students wanted to discuss their own definitions of drama, and she wanted to know more about their experiences with it.

"Please take out some paper, and write about a time when you or someone you know experienced drama." She wrote the prompt on the board as she spoke. To her surprise she didn't hear any groans from any of the students. Satisfied with her writing, she turned back to face the students.

Franklin, a gothic boy with blonde stringy hair, lifted one finger in the air.

Jada forced a smile, knowing that this would be just another day when the boy questioned her classroom exercises. Last time, he had refused to do any of the work, and she had spoken to his parents, who basically told her that he didn't garner much respect for female teachers, especially black ones like her. Jada had been blown away by their frankness and their nonchalant attitude in implicating themselves in his prejudice and chauvinistic behavior. She'd gotten to the point of just writing him up and sending him out of the class when he made offensive comments. "Yes, Franklin?"

"I don't understand why we have to do this." He drawled, the confederate flag on his jacket wrinkling with every movement.

"Well, it helps me to see what your definition of drama is, since that's our next unit, and I get to know you more through your experiences." She shuffled the papers around on her podium.

"I mean, yeaahh, but what if you never had drama?" His blue eyes flashed with challenge.

"Frank, man, just write the paragraph." Chris hissed at him.

"You don't tell me what to do." He looked back at Jada expectantly.

"The prompt asks you to write about yourself or someone you know. I'm sure you've often witnessed it in school."

"Well, when you came there was drama."

"See, write about that." Jada knew that his comment was intended to be an insult towards her, but over the past month, she had learned to ignore the students' jabs at her. There was always a student somehow indirectly referring to her weight or her clothes, or the more popular topic, her unwarranted presence. As long as they weren't being blatantly disrespectful, she chalked it up to their age.

"What if I write about how black people shouldn't complain about the confederate flag or even slavery?" He glared at her under blonde eyelashes. "That's how they got the American dream."

"Whoa! Franklin you are out of line!" Chris explained.

"White boy gone get his head beat." Another boy yelled from across the room.

Samantha, or Sam as she liked to be called, quietly spoke up again. "See, this, right now, is drama that he is trying to cause. Franklin, man, you really need to watch what you say."

"I have freedom of speech!" the boy shouted.

Jada leaned on the podium. She spoke calmly, "Okay, everyone let's calm down. Now Franklin," she turned her attention to the reddening boy. "First, I need for you to keep your voice very low. Secondly, I believe that you have been misinformed. There was nothing dreamy about slavery for several reasons. We've discussed them in this class, remember?"

"My granddad told me not to listen to that garbage 'cause all teachers do is lie!" He kicked his foot up into a desk in front of him. "Especially the black ones."

The hairs on the back of Jada's neck prickled. She rubbed them, hoping it would ease her annoyance. She'd tried multiple times through various lessons to give the boy a different point of view, and at one point, it seemed to have worked, but then he'd returned to school the next day even more defiant than he had been before. She couldn't help but feel that his parents played a huge role in it. "Well, Franklin, life will teach you so many lessons. One thing I know is that you will not disrespect me or your other classmates any longer. So, I ask that you return to your journal prompt."

"I ain't doing squat!" He kicked the legs of the desk in front of him and slammed his notebook closed.

"Frankie," a white girl pulled on his jacket, attempting to calm him.

"Mr. Singleton, you may leave the room." Jada slowly unfolded her body and placed one hand on her hip.

"I ain't gotta leave." He crossed his arms over his chest.

Jada chuckled softly. "Oh, you're gonna leave today." She walked over and pressed the office call button. She strolled back to the podium, flipping through her gradebook for the referral forms.

The boy rose from his seat and yanked his book bag over his shoulder. He walked slowly as if proving a point. The students murmured throughout the room. Jada watched him out of the corner of her eye. Just as she found the referral forms, the boy reached for her shoulder.

"See you later, teach." He shoved her against the podium.

Jada braced herself and turned to grab the boy's jacket sleeve. "Don't ever put your hands on me again." She hissed through clenched teeth, her eyes a menacing glare into the boy's own eyes. She reluctantly released the boy, regretting not pushing him back.

He gave a lopsided grin and walked out of the classroom, slamming the door behind him.

She began to write down the sequence of events on a referral slip as the students talked loudly about the boy. "Okay, get back to the free write!"

The class silenced. Montrell, a dark-skinned boy with long dreads raised his hand. "Ummm, Ms. Harris can we use what just happened for this?"

The students began to laugh. Jada found herself joining them. "If that is what you consider drama, yes, Montrell, you can use it." She smiled at him.

"Cool." He began to write vehemently.

"Ms. Harris?" Mr. Jackson stuck his head in the door.

She walked out into the hall, handing him the form and recounting the event to him.

Mr. Jackson frowned in concern. "Are you okay?"

She nodded in response.

"Good," He spoke into the walkie-talkie. "APs, we have Franklin Singleton wandering around campus. We need to find him. Bring him directly to my office if you do." He glanced out of the back door. "Ms. Allen, please call Officer James."

"Copy," they responded.

"Don't worry about it, Ms. Harris. I'll take care of it."

Jada nodded, walked into the classroom, and closed the door. "Okay, who wants to share their free write?"

Twenty-five hands shot in the air.

She shook her head and smiled. "Okay, Montrell. Let's hear it."

Chapter Nine

After the incident with Franklin, all the students seemed more protective of Jada. She still had the reputation of grading too hard and having witty comebacks for every student, but they all seemed relieved that he had been expelled indefinitely. She looked around at the students in her first period class. They were working in pairs to define Shakespearean terms for Act 1 of *Romeo and Juliet.* She'd given them a short blurb about the play, and she was surprised to find that they seemed genuinely interested in it. She noticed that many of them took on the task of defining the words as though it were a high profile case that required them to break a secret code.

"Cometh is come, fool." Ashton nudged his friend. "Fool, look at the word. It's just a weird way to say come."

"Coxcomb?" Vanessa and her partner shook their heads in bewilderment.

"Remember to use the vocabulary keys I gave you!" Jada exclaimed, walking around the room from group to group.

As they worked, she crumbled some of their old graded assignments into tiny balls. Many of them ceased their working to watch her, their eyes filled with questions. She smirked and continued to work. With each ball, she could feel the tension leaving her shoulders. It had been a month and a half, and she had experienced more than she was sure most people encountered in a year. She knew why some considered teaching to be a tough job; the students were energetic, attitudinal, and sometimes even defiant, but at the same time, they had so much charisma and, in many ways, innocence. The good moments definitely outweighed the bad ones, and every day, Jada could feel her resolve to swoop in and save them breaking down. They didn't need saving but guidance, and she was doing everything in her power to be that for them, even when they didn't want it.

After discussing their defined terms, she hauled a bucket full of wadded up paper to the front of the room. The students watched her silently. "What do you guys know about gangs?" she asked.

The class began to chatter loudly around the room. Animated murmurs about Crips, Bloods, and Gangster Disciples bounced from corner to corner.

"Whoa, whoa, whoa!" Jada held up her hands to calm them. "You guys know a lot about them."

"GD 'til I die, Ms. Harris!" Ashton began to throw up hand signs.

"Ashton, boy shut up." She put her hands on her hips. "You can't even get a J-O-B."

The class hooted in jubilation. The boy lowered his head, dragging his hand across his wavy hair and laughing softly.

"Yeen even have to do me like that, Ms. Harris!" He smirked at her.

"You did it to yourself." She pointed at him. "Now, I asked you that because *Romeo and Juliet* is about a girl and a boy being caught in the middle of two gangs and their drama. Romeo and his family are the Montagues; while, Juliet is part of the Capulets. Their love is forbidden, yet they find their way to each other anyhow."

The students listened to her intently. Demetria, who had been present much often now, seemed to hang on to every word.

"Now, when the play opens, there's a fight between the servants for each family. What does that tell you?"

Demetria raised her hand. "That their beef runs real deep, even the servants throwing 'bows."

"Correct!" Jada snapped her fingers and tapped on the girl's desk. "Obviously, they've been at war for a while now. Like you said, even the servants are in it!" Jada walked down the aisle separating the desk. Knowing that she would be teaching the play, she had rearranged the room so that half the desk was facing the other half of the desks. The students had entered the room surprised, yet excited, that they could make faces at each other from across the room. "So, we need to set the scene. I need all of you with red shirts on the left side of the room." She pointed to the desks to her left.

The students with red jumped up and hustled to the desk.

"So that means that all of you with blue shirts should sit on the right."

The students settled in their desks on opposite sides of the room.

"Red shirts you are the Capulets." She plastered a sign that read CAPULETS on the wall behind them. "And blue shirts you are the Montagues." She placed a sign behind them.

The students began to chant, making beats on their desks and sliding their shoes across the floor energetically.

"We are the Capulets, we like jets," Ashton began to rap. "Taking off like Chief Keef, no sweat. Ah, you get? I'm rapping on ya'll heads. Ya'll ain't got no clue. Lame ahh Montagues."

The class roared with laughter and applause.

"Ashton did that!" A girl yelled from across the room.

"Thank you, baby. Tickets all sold out." He grinned and leaned back in his seat, placing his pen between his lips and folding his arms behind his head.

"Thank you for the song Ashton. Now listen." Jada said. "Every day when you come in, you are to sit according to what color shirt you have on. If your uniform shirt is blue sit on the Montague side. If it's red, you are a Capulet. Got it?"

The students nodded their heads.

"Cool. Let's begin by reading the first part. I need people to volunteer to be servants who start the fight, and instead of using swords, you guys are going to have a Montague versus Capulet paper ball fight. Who wants to volunteer to read?"

Hands shot in the air.

Jada chuckled within herself. *Got 'em again*, she thought.

***

Jada snatched up the last paper ball, returning it to the bucket.

"Okay, the floor is clear. You guys can leave now. See you tomorrow."

The students filed out of the room. They looked exhausted, but they chattered excitedly about the paper ball fight and what color shirt they would wear the next day. Jada was pleased to see that they had enjoyed themselves. She could only hope that she kept them this engaged throughout the whole play. She smiled at them as they passed her, dapping the fists of those who stuck theirs out to her.

"Whew," Demetria stumbled towards her, her chubby cheeks flexed into a smile. "I'm tired after that, Ms. Harris."

"I bet you are." Jada put her hand on the girl's shoulder. "I'm happy to see you in class more."

The girl smiled at the floor, her long eyelashes dropping slowly to her cheeks. "I be having a lot going on."

Jada was alarmed by the sorrowful tone in the girl's voice. She wanted to press her for more information but figured she'd get more by remaining silent.

"Umm. I don't know how to tell you this," she shifted her weight from leg to leg. "My mom passed last year. I just been having to deal with a lot." She looked up at Jada, tears gathering in her reddened eyes.

"Oh, my. Demetria." She placed her hand on the girl's shoulder. "I had no idea. Can I hug you?"

The girl nodded stiffly.

Jada reached for her, and she seemed to fall into her arms, sobbing softly.

"I know that's hard." Jada cooed. "And I know you've already heard this, but God had a plan. He must've known that you could handle it."

"I--i-it just g-g-gets so hard." The girl blubbered, her tears flowing more rapidly. "Then, my little sister is so young, and I have to be mom now. It's just so much." She pulled her head from Jada's shoulder and wiped her eyes vigorously.

Jada sensed that crying in public made Demetria uncomfortable. "I can't stand here and say that I know how it feels because I'd be lying to you, but what I can say is that I know what it means to truly love your mother."

The girl nodded.

"And I know that if I were to lose mine, it would hurt deeply, but you're not alone. I'm here any time that you want or need to talk about whatever. During my planning period, if your teacher will let you out, you're free to come and just sit with me. Okay?"

Demetria sniffled and nodded her head. "And I'm sorry that I haven't really been in class. I j-j-just-- when that happened---it's just been hard for me to get out the bed every morning ever since."

Jada rested her hand on the girl's shoulder, looking her in her eyes, "I understand, but what would your mother want you to do?"

"Oh, she'd want me in school. She didn't play about grades and stuff."

"Right. So, you need to honor her by doing what you know she would've wanted. I can't help you if you're not here. Hmm?"

"I know. I'll be here more; I promise. The paper ball fight was more fun than I'd had in a long time. It was like a stress relief."

"Good." Jada clasped her hands beneath her chin. "I'm really happy to hear that. And remember, I'm here for you."

"Got it!" The girl readjusted her bag on her shoulder and began to walk off. Turning back to Jada, she said, "Ms. Harris, I'm glad you here. Representin' for us big girls and all, too."

"Gotta do that." Jada folded her arms over her chest and leaned against the wall, watching the girl saunter down the hall.

She thought of her own mother, whom she hadn't seen very much of lately. Usually she didn't leave the school until an hour after dismissal due to bus duty. And even once she returned home, her nights were filled with preparing for class the next day and grading papers. When her mother had called, Jada had offered short answers or rushed her off the phone, and now she felt guilty. She made a mental note to stop by the house on her way home and check on her.

***

"Hi, mama's baby!" Her mother pulled her into the dimly lit home and into a warm embrace. "You need to eat something. You're losing weight on me! Are you eating lunch?" Her mother looked genuinely concerned, lines sketched in her forehead. She watched Jada closely.

"Most days, I eat. Sometimes, I don't have time." She loosened her scarf and pulled it from around her neck.

"How come?" Her mother asked, ushering her into the living room.

"Well, sometimes, I take that time to call parents, knowing that they're probably on lunch, too, or I get caught up grading papers or talking to a student."

Her mom squinted her eyes at her. "That is no excuse. You can't let this school kill you, Jada." She stood slowly, wiped her hands down her skirt and strolled into the kitchen.

"I know, mama. I'll do better."

"Yes, you will. Starting now." She reached into one of the cupboards and grabbed a black ceramic bowl. She walked over to the stove, and stirred whatever was in the pot with a wooden spoon.

"Mom," she stood. "What are you cooking?"

"My vegetable soup and grilled cheese sandwiches." She smiled, looking at Jada out of the corner of her eye.

Jada's stomach began to growl loudly. "Oh, that sounds so good."

"Mhm. Sit down and I'll fix you some." She began filling the bowl with soup. "What's been going on at that school besides you not eating?"

"Oh, so much, Ma." Jada sighed. "The students are so, so--" she struggled to find an accurate word to describe them. "They're so funny, and mischievous and smart. Like they know about more things than what I knew at their age. Half the time, *I'm* the one blushing. It's crazy. And you can tell that at home, most of them are treated like adults. They don't have traditional parents."

Her mother placed the tray with grilled cheese and a bowl of soup on her lap.

"Mmm. Ma, this looks and smells so good." She sipped a spoonful of the soup, followed by the grilled cheese, and felt that she would faint from utter fulfillment. "Oh, my God. This is so good," she mumbled between slurps.

"Good. Now, slow down and finish telling me about work."

"Oh, yeah, well. I have a few students who are just characters. There's this boy named Ashton in my first period class, and he is such a clown, but a really good kid. He brings so much fun and energy to the room, but there's this one teacher who is always writing him up. I just don't get it. I've never had any real problems out of him." She took another sip of soup. "It seems like his suspensions are getting longer and longer. And it's all because of tardies and or speaking out of turn in her class."

"Maybe she just doesn't like him." Her mother passed her a napkin.

Jada wiped some soup from the corner of her lips. "That's what I've been thinking. Sometimes, it seems like she's looking for things to write him up for. I don't know what to do."

"You seem to have a good rapport with the principal. Why don't you speak to him about it?"

"You're talking about Mr. Jackson. Mr. Dennis, the Assistant Principal, is the one over discipline." She sat the spoon on the plate. "I don't know about him. He's a bit too flirty for me."

"Isn't he married?" Her mom came and grabbed the tray from her lap.

Jada leaned back on the couch. "Yes, ma'am. But what does that mean nowadays?"

Her mom offered her a knowing smirk, reclining in the chair Jada had bought her for Christmas. "Yeah, buddy. You're right about that one. Are you sure it's flirting?"

Jada leaned forward. "Okay, so the other day I'm walking to my bus duty post, and all of a sudden from behind me, I hear." She placed her fingers between her lips and whistled. "Then, he yelled, "Ooo-wee. I sure like your boooot-s, Ms. Harris.""

Confusion registered across her mother's face. "Okay, and?"

"No, mom. You don't get it. I was walking ahead of him in some basic boots. When he said the word 'boots,' it was clear to me that he wasn't really talking about the boots. Then, he came outside and started asking me about what I do on the weekends and stuff, all up in my personal space. Like, it just didn't feel professional."

"Okay, well, if you say it didn't then it didn't. You should report him."

"See, but I'm worried that I'll get the same response that you had in the beginning. I need to be sure."

"Okay, I see." She placed her hands atop her rising stomach. "But you don't let any man say what he wants to you. You understand?"

"Oh, of course, mama." She stared at the floor thoughtfully. "Oh! And you remember the little girl that got her menstrual cycle at school?"

Her mom stared back at her blankly. "No! Wow, that's one thing I prayed for for my girls, and all of you got yours at home." She raised her hand towards Heaven.

"I know, but long story short, she got her cycle, and I ran around making sure she had everything she needed. Her mom came up to the school and snapped because she felt that I'd overstepped my bounds."

"Really?! For giving her child a pad?!" Her mom looked confused.

"Yes! But that's not even the worst part." She sat up, planting her feet firmly on the hardwood floor. "That happened almost two months ago, and now, the girl is pregnant!"

"Oh my! Pregnant at 14 years old? Do you teach the little boy, too?"

Jada answered softly. "Here's the thing with that. I'm hearing that she's pregnant by a grown man."

Her mother shook her head vigorously. "Jada, tell me you're lying. That's disgusting. She's a child!"

"I know, Mama. I ju-just haven't been able to wrap my head around it. I still don't know if it's true or not, but the kids have been talking non-stop. I have to threaten them with extra work to quiet them down about it."

"You have a relationship with her now. Have you tried talking to her?"

"I have. She will only confirm that she's pregnant, but she anxiously skirts around any questions about the baby's father. I've just been trying to be supportive and comforting because she's scared."

"I can imagine. I mean, she just got her cycle! To go from that to being pregnant just sounds absurd."

"That's exactly what went through my head when she told me. The crazy thing is that her mom doesn't seem to be very concerned about it." She sighed loudly.

"That's a lot, Jada, but if in helping her you find yourself needing support, you can always reach out to me. I know what it's like being a first time mom." She rubbed her arms and offered a slight smile. "But now, tell me how are *you* doing?" Her mother's stare burned a hole into Jada. She shifted uncomfortably on the couch, lacing her fingers together atop one knee.

"I'm okay, just exhausted." She sighed heavily. "You know, when you're going through the process and stuff, they don't tell you how tired you'll be, or all that you'll have to do as a teacher. I wasn't professionally prepared for all this. Most of it is coming from my own experience as a student and your oldest child. Like, many days, I don't feel like just a teacher. I feel like a nanny, and then, many parents make their grand appearances at odd times, not when you've called them about their child's performance or behavior. Oh no, they show up when the child has been suspended. Why? Because half the time, they don't want the child at home with them. How ridiculous does that sound?"

Her mom shook her head and rolled her eyes toward the ceiling. "Sounds very ridiculous. I didn't want you guys suspended because you'd miss work; it never had anything to do with me wanting free time. I worked. Wait, these parents don't have jobs?"

Jada shot her a sarcastic smirk. "Many sit around and collect welfare. Not all, but several do. And the crazy thing is that the kids come to school bragging about it. It's like a goal or something."

Her mother shook her head in disbelief. "Wow. Well, that's why you're there to show them something different."

"Well, yeah, but at the same time, parents come in calling me bougie and uppity, and you can just tell that they sit around and put it in the kids' heads, too. Like, one day, I'll have a good day with some of them, and then, the next day, they'll come in all resistant and with a wall up, and I have to start all the way over with them. It's draining." She stretched out on the plush, tan sofa, her arm behind her head.

"Remember that you're still new, and you're coming in during the middle of the year. You can't expect all of them to warm up to you right away. Also, remember that they had half a year of coming in and doing nothing but getting A's, and now, you're coming in working them in ways that they didn't have to before. Unfortunately, students don't like the teacher who teaches."

Jada grunted. "You sure know what to say, Mama." She pulled the blanket from the back of the couch. "You remember how I would run home and tell you if a teacher showed us movies every day?"

Her mom nodded with a half-smile. "I sure do."

"Well, these kids do the opposite; they run home and tell their parents if you're not showing movies and giving A's all day." She placed her arm over her eyes. "Good kids just screwed up priorities." She yawned.

"That's a shame." Her mother shook her head. "When I was in high school in Chicago, they didn't introduce black students to nursing and well-paying careers. You wanna know what they encouraged us to become?"

Jada raised her eyebrow, urging her to continue.

"Secretaries and assistants for girls, and they encouraged boys to work in factories or be athletes. I would have loved to have a teacher like you who really challenged me."

"Awe. Thanks, mom." Jada blew a kiss at her. "You sure know what to say to a girl."

"Well, now that I've buttered you up, how's Caleb?" Her mother asked softly.

"Hmph. He's not." She peeked at her mother from under her arm, hoping she'd get the hint to drop the subject. She didn't.

"You know, I like him. He's a good boy, but sometimes, good just isn't good enough."

Jada nodded slowly, her eyelids growing heavy as her thoughts shifted to Caleb. *What's he doing? Who's he doing it with? Was he thinking about her?* She couldn't be sure that she'd given him much thought lately, being that most of her days were filled with emotional students and combative parents. She had to admit that a few times she wondered if maybe he'd done her a favor. She no longer had to argue about not spending enough time talking to him throughout the day or being too busy. She didn't *have* to talk to anyone everyday if she didn't want to. She smiled before drifting off to sleep.

Chapter Ten

The streets were blanketed in white. Icicles hung from each of the two-story houses that lined the short suburban street. Jada tiptoed from the drafty window and snatched up the remote control from the sofa, flipping on the T.V. and turning to the news. She nearly jumped out of her socks when she saw that the high school would be closed due to the snow. Easing back onto the sofa covered in blankets, she stared at the line of words that ran across the screen announcing all of the school closures. She hadn't expected to spend the night at her mother's house, but it couldn't have happened at a better time. She'd wanted to take a day off since the second full week of school, but she could never bring herself to submit the paperwork.

She lay back on the couch, elated, not sure what she'd do with the rest of the day, but sure that her body would thank her later.

"Good morning, Mama's baby." Her mother strolled into the living room, planting a kiss on her forehead. She glanced at the time at the bottom of the screen. "Shouldn't you be getting ready for work?"

"Yes ma'am, but it's snowing; so, no school."

"Oh, good for you. You need the rest." Her mother made busy fixing coffee in the kitchen.

"I know. I'm not complaining."

"I wouldn't either. Well, why don't you go up to your old room and get in the bed?"

"You know what, I will." She stood, yanking the blanket and pillow off the couch and dragged her plush body up the stairs.

Inside, she was rejoicing like it was the last day of the month, payday. She frowned when thoughts of her syllabus flashed in her mind. She would have to push back or reschedule everything, but it was just a day. She was sure she could improvise without issue. She sprinted down the hall and into her old room, each wall flanked with large posters of Outkast, Tyrese, Chingy, Chris Brown, and Ludacris. She chuckled at one time being deeply in love---well, she thought--- with each of them and their music. A dry erase board adorned the wall perpendicular to her window. College acceptance letters, her gold navy blue graduation cords, and pictures of her former high school buddies surrounded the board.

Fingering the dusty films, she remembered all the time she spent crying and worrying about her weight as a young child. She'd spend countless hours shifting from side to side in front of the mirror, critiquing the narrowness of her hips and her petite breasts, or the way her stomach managed to overlap her waist line. Bumps spread rapidly on her chubby face, and her braces sparkled under the glare of light from overhead. She'd sit and critique herself in ways that she knew her peers would, but she felt that as long as she beat them to the insults, she wouldn't be surprised by them. She was often wrong, as they usually came up with some nickname or some derogatory statement that she hadn't prepared for. And she'd sat in a self-hating funk for a good amount of time, but it had been her mother who forced her to confront her bullies and insecurities. She chuckled to herself as she thought about dissing sessions with her mom.

"When she say something to you, you say, 'I might be chubby, but you can build a bridge between your two front teeth and take it all the way to New York.'" Then, her mother would tell her to repeat it with as much sass as she'd heard it.

Jada would recite it, her chubby finger wagging in the air and her neck moving from side to side.

Her mother would rock back and forth on the bed, laughing, and then she'd raise her hand high for Jada to reach up and give her a high five. She'd remind Jada that fighting was an absolute last resort, but that words, oh words had power, and ever since then, she'd relied on them heavily.

Now, she realized that this is what prompted her love for words and all that they could do. In essence, words had prompted her to be a teacher, when her white, fourth grade teacher whispered doubt in her ear, reminding her that she was the only black child in the class and that her skills were considered subpar to everyone else's. She'd made up her mind that day to become an English teacher, and she'd held steadfast to that goal. She'd built up her confidence by 'faking it 'til she made it,' and now, at 24 years old, she was proud of herself.

She placed the National Honor Society trophy back on the shelf and smoothed the sheets on the bed before jumping joyfully beneath the comforter. She began to fall into a deep trance-like sleep, but it was interrupted by the uncontrollable buzzing of her phone. Notifications filtered in back to back. Finally, she was able to open one of the news alerts.

CALDWIN HIGH SCHOOL TEACHER ACCUSED OF IMPREGNATING 14-YEAR-OLD STUDENT

Jada quickly exited the screen and opened her message inbox. Texts from her co-workers popped up, repeating what she already knew. She hesitantly opened the group chat with Mr. Williams and the others that had joined them for dinner to find a huge picture of Coach Young, smirking back at her. Beneath his picture were messages from various teachers who swore they knew it well in advance but had not been confident enough to speak on it. Jada signed out of the app and made a beeline for the news report.

She read it in shock. According to the report, the students' mother had found the pair outside her house, in the teacher's car at which time the student revealed that the teacher had coerced her into having sex with him for the past year. Jada noticed a video and clicked the play button. Her heart sank as her suspicion was confirmed. On the screen, was Vanessa's mom discussing how Coach Young had coerced the girl by threatening not to help her with tests and homework. She went on to explain that he'd kept the girl quiet by showering her with gifts and at times, doing her work for her.

Jada felt nauseated. She'd heard of these ordeals, but never had she imagined that she'd be so close to it. She felt dirty, as if she had been complicit in Coach Young's scheme. In her mind, she replayed all of the conversations she'd had with him about Vanessa. Yes, there had been signs. She remembered the way Vanessa would instantly become humble whenever his name was mentioned. A lump formed in Jada's throat; she couldn't breathe. The muscles in her neck tightened, and her mouth went dry. She felt the urge to scream, but she didn't know where it would come from. She couldn't help but feel that she should've noticed sooner, that she should have asked Vanessa more questions, or listened to her more closely. She should've, she just should have....

Chapter Eleven

The hallways buzzed with incessant chatter and laughter. After two weeks' worth of snow days, classes were resuming, and the students had received an immense amount of energy that surprised Jada. She'd expected them to enter the school building dragging their feet with depressed frowns and upturned noses, but they'd practically broken down the door to get inside. Jada assumed that it had something to do with the scandal that hung over the school.

"Girl, Coach Young was pimpin' that girl!" one student said, between bubblegum bubbles and popping.

"Ha mama shoulda knew!" another girl yelled.

"Mane, I heard her mama knew the whole time, and he was giving her stuff, too." A boy added.

"Fool, me too. I bet he was wit 'em both."

Jada clapped her hands very loud to signal her disapproval. The chatter instantly stopped and the foursome hurried to their classes. She felt that she would have to do that all day, and she wasn't looking forward to it. As the students filed into her classroom, she searched the halls for Vanessa. She hoped that she wouldn't be at school today. She could only imagine the embarrassment she felt, especially being that her mother had all but revealed her name during the news report. If there could have been any speculation, she'd ruined any chance of it, and now, all of the students were weighing in on the issue with a massive amount of "he said, she said." Jada said a quick prayer that Vanessa would find peace.

"You're too pretty to be frowning." The flash of Coach Lewis' fake tooth yanked Jada out of her prayer.

She continued to frown at him. "How can I help you, Coach?"

"Well, we're so formal. Madam, I was just speaking." He offered an exaggerated bow at the waist.

Jada rolled her eyes. "I'm really not in the mood."

"Who got your panties in a wad?" He playfully punched her arm.

She cut her eyes at him sharply. "How can you even try to play right now? Your homeboy was caught sleeping with a student."

His eyes lowered to the floor, and he scratched his temple nervously. "Yeah. It's crazy, but you don't understand."

She crossed her arms over her chest tightly, tilting her chin to look him in the eye. "What do you mean? What is there to understand? He basically raped a 14-year-old?"

"Whoa! I hadn't read any reports that said raped." His wide chest fell and rose quickly in front of her.

"Tell me you're not defending him!" Her eyes stared back at him, accusingly.

"I'm not; all I'm saying is that he made a mistake. Man, these 14-year-olds don't look like 14-year-olds anymore. They'll try to come at you like grown women."

"So, you're a grown man. It's called *self*-control. It's your job to put them in their place." She pushed a stray hair out of her face and tucked it behind her ear. "Like, I don't understand. If that is what happened, how hard is it to say no?!"

"No if about it. That is what happened. He told me when she first tried him, walking into the room one day, trying to sit on his lap and stuff. He pushed her off, but she kept trying. I guess he couldn't fight her off anymore."

"So, why didn't he go report it to Mr. Jackson?"

"He wanted to, but she said that if he told, she'd claim he forced her into having sex with him. So, he had to buy her gifts and do her work and stuff to keep her from lyin' on him. These young girls aren't regular little girls, Ms. Harris."

"I don't believe any of it. I think he fed you that crap to cover himself. How do I know you didn't know about it the whole time?" She stepped closer to him, her chest mere inches from his.

He fingered the whistle hanging from his neck. "Because if I did, I'd be on the news, too. You don't think the police would've uncovered that by now? The reality is that most of these little girls just as loose as some of these teachers. " He sneakily glanced up and down the hall.

She looked away, greeting a few of the students as they entered the room. "I don't know about all that." She thought of all the times that she'd commented on how friendly Coach Lewis was with the female students. Everyone had chalked it up to him having been a teacher and coach for the school for numerous years, but still that didn't explain why he seemed to be so comfortable with the girls. It made Jada uncomfortable.

Staring at him now, she made a silent vow to keep a close eye on him so that she wouldn't make the same mistake again. She refused to have another one of her students be a victim to the likes of Coach Young. She wasn't convinced that Vanessa had asked for her current circumstances. Her overall demeanor did not line up with the image that Coach Lewis was painting.

The bell to start first period rang. "I have to go." She left Coach Lewis standing in the hall and walked into the classroom that was alert with whispers and rapid murmurs. She closed the door and locked it, wishing she could do the same with the thoughts of Vanessa.

***

Demetria plopped her tray with dried up cheese pizza and corn on the table, as she sat beside Jada in the busy cafeteria.

"What's up, Ms. Harris?" she said, popping a spoon full of corn in her mouth.

"Not a thing, chicken wing. What's going on with you?"

"Same. Just trying to live life."

"And how's that going?" Jada scooped some pears into her mouth, staring back at the girl.

"It's better now." Demetria spoke softly.

"Oh, yeah? What's making it better?" She glanced around the lunch room, as students traded milk for pizza slices or asked each other for a dollar to buy ice cream.

"You. Meeting you has made it so much better." She lowered her eyelashes and fumbled with her hands under the table.

Jada was taken aback by the girl's comment. It had only been two months, and yet, she felt a kinship to the girl as well. She reminded her so much of herself, and Jada had made it a point to tell her that on several occasions. She looped her arm over the girl's shoulder and pulled her close in a side hug.

"I feel the same about you, my girl!" She squeezed the girl tightly against her side.

Jada cared deeply for Demetria. It hadn't been hard to love her spirit, her drive, the way she appeared so strong; yet, Jada knew that she was softer and more vulnerable than she let on to others. But Jada had seen at times, the sadness that flashed in her eyes whenever a student mentioned his or her mother, or the way that she nervously lowered her eyes, battered her long eyelashes, and twirled her hair around her finger whenever someone offered her a compliment. But she'd also noticed the way that she doted on her younger sister, asking her about and checking on her grades, ensuring that she made it to school safely, and getting her hair styled regularly, while still dragging herself to school. Jada, the eldest of her mother's children, had stepped up and helped her own younger siblings as her mother completed nursing school, trading in some night's out with friends for homework tutoring; so, she found that, to some degree, she could identify with Demetria. Quite frankly, Demetria seemed to be doing better than most of the parents Jada had met. And it didn't hurt that she was also a plus size girl.

The girl beamed back at her before biting the pizza.

Jada nudged her playfully and took a hefty bite of her turkey sandwich.

"Ms. Harris, can I see you in my office?" Mr. Jackson, the principal, knocked gently on the table.

Jada nodded, her cheeks stuffed with food. She worked hard to chew up the sandwich and swallow before standing, gathering her lunch box and keys, and exchanging glances with Demetria. She followed behind Mr. Jackson as they entered his cold office.

"Please, have a seat." He said, sweeping his hands toward the chair across from his hollow, oak desk.

Jada sat slowly, tucking her skirt securely under her legs.

"I know it's almost March and that it might be too soon, but I would like to speak with you about next year."

Jada nodded, "Okay." She laced her fingers together tightly. "What about next year?"

"Well, I've visited your classroom, and I hear so much about your teaching. The 9th graders have definitely made some strides in such a short amount of time." He shuffled some paper around on his desk. "Now, of course, I've heard the good and the bad. They think you're too hard, but I also see how they rush to get to your class on time. When they leave out of your classroom, they're smiling and laughing, or talking about what they've done. I really need that in every class."

Jada felt that she would explode, as he rambled on and on about each of her classes. She was anxious to know why he'd called her into the office, especially during lunch. Her stomach growled in agreement.

"Well, I believe we need the same kind of rigor, if not more, for seniors. So I would like to know if you would be interested in teaching senior English next school year? I would also like for you to teach a senior Advanced Placement class and become the new PLC leader."

"Wow," she whispered. Jada placed her hand over her stomach to ensure that she was still breathing. "B-but, I'm still in my first year."

"Yeah, but let me tell you. You are a natural. It's so easy for me to forget that you are a first-year teacher; you came in demanding respect, and the students know it. The difference you've made in this 9th grade class has been outstanding. I can only imagine what you'll bring to next year's seniors, who are entitled and rambunctious. They need a strong teacher like you who will challenge them in ways that other teachers have not been able to. You know they ran off their English teacher this year?"

"Yes, I'd heard." She nodded stiffly.

"So, that should tell you. Plus, you're innovative, knowledgeable, and your classroom management has been impeccable. I think you'd do well with them. So what do you say?"

He flashed a white grin, intertwining his fingers and placing his hands atop his protruding stomach.

Jada hadn't noticed his belly before, maybe because of the loud colors he usually wore. But today, he was subtle in a black collar shirt, a red and white plaid, sweater vest, and a red bow tie. The colors popped against his dark skin. Jada turned her attention to his offer. It was more along the lines of what she wanted when she'd first applied to work at the school, except she'd wanted to teach 11th grade. While she'd been slightly disappointed when they'd offered her the 9th grade teaching position, she'd understood their decision, as it allowed her to become better acclimated to the demands of students.

"Does moving up come with a pay raise?"

"I thought you'd never ask. Yes, it does. Now, because it's your first year, it's not a significant raise, more like a few hundred dollars plus a couple more hundreds for being AP certified and the PLC leader. The more years of experience you get, the greater your raise will be."

"Okay, and what will I have to do to become AP certified?" She fumbled with the keys sitting in her lap.

He pulled some papers out of a folder. "There's a one week seminar you'll attend over the Summer just forty-five minutes up the road in Somerset. We'll cover your gas mileage as well as your hotel expenses."

It was too much for Jada to take in at once, her head was swirling with ideas and ways that she could teach the senior class. Not to mention, a few hundreds would definitely help. Her only fear was that she would get in over her head. She didn't want to fail.

As if reading her mind, Mr. Jackson spoke, "You're a great teacher, Ms. Harris. No amount of years can take that from you. Now, I've already spoken to Mr. Keystone and asked him about teaching 9th grade so that you can work with the seniors; he was okay with it. And Ms. Calloway has already assured me that she'll work with you to develop your skills as the new PLC leader, so I'm not leaving you out in the middle of nowhere alone. I'll help you in every way that I can." He smiled back at her.

Jada mulled over his words silently. Caleb flashed into her mind and just as quickly disappeared. "I'll do it." Her voice caught her by surprise. She smiled nervously.

Mr. Jackson clapped his palms together and stood. "I'm so happy to hear that. You'll be great." He walked around the desk, squeezed her shoulder softly, and handed her the folder full of papers. "Everything you need is in this folder. We're so glad to have you."

"Glad to be here. Thank you, Mr. Jackson." She tucked the folder under her arms and made her way towards the door. "Oh, Mr. Jackson?" She stopped, turning towards him. "Have you heard anything about Vanessa?"

He shoved his hands into his pockets. "Yes, I spoke with her mother briefly this morning. She plans to withdraw Vanessa from the school. She says that Vanessa doesn't want to return to school, too embarrassed, and to be honest with you, Ms. Harris, considering all the chatter, I don't blame her."

"Yeah, neither do I. I just hate it for her. Any word on Coach Young?"

He sighed heavily, before returning to his seat and crossing his legs at the ankle. "Well, he's out on a $15,000 bail. He won't be teaching here any longer." He placed a finger on his temple.

"Okay, thanks."
Jada seemed to float from his office and back toward her classroom. She hadn't imagined that she'd so quickly move up the ladder, but

she was honored that out of all of the English teachers, he'd asked her, the least experienced of them all. Her mother's words since she was a child echoed in her head, *You were born to be a teacher.* Ever since she'd told her mom that she wanted to be a teacher in fourth grade, she had reassured her that being a teacher was her calling. And now, Jada knew that her purpose in life had been confirmed. She'd heard about terrible, power-hungry principals, but Mr. Jackson defied everything she'd imagined. As a principal, he was attentive, friendly, innovative, and opportunistic. He didn't demean them in faculty meetings or make offensive demands. As a first-year teacher, she couldn't have asked for a better principal.

Ms. Calloway rounded the corner. "Based on that smile, I take it that Mr. Jackson spoke with you about next year."

"He did," Jada said, startled. She didn't know she'd been smiling.

"Well, I hope you're ready to work. Those kids are spoiled rotten." She placed her hand on her hip.

"He alluded to that." Jada couldn't help but feel slightly nervous.

"And then, you're a first-year teacher. They're going to try to run all over you." The woman stared intensely back at her.

"I'm sure they will, but it's nothing I can't handle." She smiled back at her, challenging the woman to continue on her mission to discourage her.

She accepted the challenge. "Iiii don't know. They ran off the last teacher."

"Yep. Heard that one, too. But have you, as an instructional facilitator ever thought about the fact that maybe there was more *you* could've done to help her? Maybe the kids didn't run her off, perhaps the lack of support did." Jada raised her eyebrow and crossed her arms.

Ms. Calloway shifted in her stance. "No, she was just weak. But I'm here to assist you in any way you need it. Just the say the word." She strolled away and closed her office door loudly.

Ever since she'd gone out to dinner with them, Ms. Calloway had been giving her the cold shoulder. It wasn't as if she'd ever been very friendly to Jada, but she was definitely colder.

Jada shrugged off their depressing conversation and walked quickly to her room, hoping to have her excitement contained by the time the lunch bell rang.

Chapter Twelve

"Ladies and gentlemen, we're halfway through the semester." Mr. Jackson clapped his hands thunderously.

Applause sounded around the room, followed by hoots and hollers. The teachers began to murmur about Spring Break.

"Baaayby, I can't wait to stick these toes in the sand." Mrs. Inglewood, the Computer teacher said, high-fiving Ms. Henson, the guidance counselor.

"You," Ms. Henson gave her a sideways smirk. "Ima go and turn my phone all the way off."

The table laughed loudly.

"Yes, yes. You all should be very excited. As we close out the first 9 weeks, I'd like to announce the winners of our hallway competition." He glanced around the room. "The assistant principals and I have been talking and paying very close attention to the amount of students in the halls between classes and after the tardy bell, and I want to thank each of you, but there was one hall that really buckled down and helped us a lot."

Mr. Rucker, the white assistant principal simulated a drum roll on the library table.

"And the winner is," Mr. Jackson paused dramatically. "Hall B!"

Jada and her hall mates beamed with pride. There was no doubt in her minds that they'd be the winners, with her loud voice and Mrs. Akins' squeaky one, most of the students avoided them like the plague, and it helped that their classrooms were located at opposite ends of the hall, so usually, what slipped past one of them, was caught by the other.

"As promised, you all will receive a dinner on us." He gestured toward the assistant principals. "Mr. Rucker is handling the menu and everything. Right, Doc?"

"Sure thing," the assistant principal offered a salute.

Jada smiled back at him. She hadn't seen him wandering the halls often, but being the only white administrator in the school, he seemed fairly comfortable. A goofy grin was always plastered on his face, and Jada couldn't remember a time when she'd ever seen him angry. In essence, he seemed to be a great balance between Mr.

Jackson and Mr. Dennis. Other than wanting him to be more visible, Jada didn't have very many complaints about him.

"Good thing. Hall B, we will host the dinner at the close of this week so, next Friday. I just want to thank all of you for participating. We're already working on the competition for 4th 9 weeks." Mr. Jackson stuck his hands in his pockets. "Now, a few housekeeping things. First, I want to address the rumors that have been circulating all day by letting you all know that Coach Young will not be returning. According to the Caldwin Police Department, both he and Vanessa are missing. Her mother believes that they've run away together. I wanted to inform you before you go home and see it on the 5 o'clock news."

Murmurs broke out all over the room. Jada bounced her knee nervously under the table as she bit her bottom lip. She still found it hard to believe that Vanessa had bullied Coach Young into sleeping with her.

"Wait. Everyone calm down." He patted the air with both hands. "Now, I told you all of that in confidence. I expect that none of you will go and gossip about the situation with students. That's partly the reason why so many students are so aware of this situation. Please refrain from sitting around discussing these matters with the students. That's not why you are here." He looked at each of them over the rim of his glasses. "Are there any questions?"

Jada raised her hand. "Is she in danger?"

"Well, to answer your question, I'll say this: The restraining order against Coach Young was dropped by her mother yesterday; CPD has no reason to believe that she is in danger at this time. They believe it is consensual and that her mother was aware. Now, I have invited Iman Sufora to our faculty meeting today to discuss the appropriate behaviors and interactions we should have with our students. She is a sexual harassment consultant." He snatched his glasses off his face and folded them in his hands. "I asked her to come because I want all of us to be aware of the severity of this situation and to avoid it at all costs. To engage in an inappropriate relationship of any kind with a student is unacceptable." He stared at them before yielding the floor to the consultant, who walked briskly to the front of the room and pulled her presentation up on the screen.

Jada's mind drifted from the room and back into the girl's restroom on the day that she forged a relationship with Vanessa. After that, the girl had remained relatively close to Jada throughout the school day, popping in at random times to speak or ask if she needed any assistance. Jada had seen her flourish, and she'd been proud, but now, she wondered if the girl had been feigning weakness the whole time. Jada shook the thought out of her head, knowing that even if she had been pretending, there was still some sort of insecurity or problem that would cause her to turn to someone more than twice her age. Jada murmured another quick prayer for the girl's safety, before tuning back into the presentation.

"It is not okay to touch students. If you're going to touch them, you need to ask. So, say, for instance, that a student did well on a quiz. Before you rub his arm, ask them, 'Is it okay if I touch you?'" The woman demonstrated the gesture on Mr. Jackson.

Jada stifled a chuckle at the utter ridiculousness of her suggestion. It actually sounded much more perverted than just patting the student's hand. She couldn't imagine saying that to a student. She began to doodle on the meeting agenda in front of her; she was beyond ready for Spring Break.

***

Fastening her seatbelt, Jada thought of all the sleep she was about to get this week. She glanced in the rearview mirror, glimpsing sight of Mrs. Kimble in a tight red pencil skirt, a white sheer blouse, and nude stiletto pumps. She nervously glanced around before entering the fieldhouse.

Jada shook her head and yanked the gear into reverse. *There is enough freakiness going on already*, she thought. She couldn't imagine what she and her husband got out of sexing in a dirty, stinky football lounge. She shrugged before placing her arm behind the passenger seat and turning to look out the rear window to back out of her parking space. She slammed on the breaks as she watched Coach

Lewis lazily saunter towards the fieldhouse. He opened the door, looked about nervously, before entering and closing the door softly behind him.

Jada felt like her eyes would fall out of her skull. She slowly turned back towards the front, placing her hands at 10 and 2 on the steering wheel. She heaved a long sigh after what felt like years of not breathing. She thought back to her conversation with Coach Lewis when he'd said that many of the teachers were loose. He'd been talking about Mrs. Kimble! The married Mrs. Kimble! Wait, they were both married. Jada was sure that in the last two weeks, she had seen and heard it all. This Spring Break was definitely needed!

***

Caleb's number flashed across her screen. Jada stared down at the illuminated screen. The last time she'd spoken to him, they'd agreed to go their separate ways, at least until he had developed some hint of a career path. The past few weeks had been full of the waiting game, and now that he was calling, she wasn't sure that she wanted to answer, especially not on the first day of her Spring Break. She highly doubted that he would have a definite set of goals in such a short amount of time. Her phone registered the missed call, sending him to voicemail. She waited a few minutes to see if he would leave a voicemail, but there was nothing. She wondered if he'd call back.

Ten minutes had passed, and still nothing. She pumped her fist in the air, happy that she didn't feel as nostalgic as she had in the past. She was growing more comfortable not talking to him every day, and that, within itself, was worthy of celebration.

She rushed to print her plane ticket and dialed her friend, Lena. She hadn't gone out of town for Spring Break since undergrad, and she was absolutely stoked that in less than four hours they would be landing in their old stomping grounds of St. Louis, Missouri. The embedded historical artifacts and scenery had always intrigued Jada, and because Lena was a budding archaeologist, it made her a pleasant travel companion.

Jada grabbed her keys off the table in the foyer before rushing out and closing the door loudly behind her.

Chapter Thirteen

Jada yawned for the third time since entering the school. St. Louis had been everything she'd needed. She smiled down at her buzzing cellphone, alerting her to a new text message. It was Johnathan, an art teacher she'd met at an art museum while touring the city. She'd been walking around, snapping pictures when he walked up, startling her in mid-snap.

"You know, a phone does art no justice." His voice was deep, dripping with sweetness.

Jada knew that she should've been worried, but she'd only heard kindness, and the catch in breath was the only indication of his nervousness. She turned to face him.

His eyes were dark and seductive, framed by long eyelashes and set in an almond-colored face. His hair was low-cut and rippled with soft waves. He smiled beautifully, a finely-groomed goatee surrounding his full lips.

Jada licked her lips slowly, her mouth becoming dry instantly. She hadn't expected to be so very attracted to him; she mentally fussed over her hair. *Did she have lipstick on her teeth? Was her breath fresh?* She tucked her hair, nervously, behind her ear. "Well, everyone isn't fortunate enough to have a fancy camera." She gestured towards the compact, black camera hanging from his neck.

He chuckled. "Well, that's why you have to hang with someone who does." He winked at her, mischievously. "Hi, I'm Johnathan." He stuck his hand out towards her.

"Nice to meet you. I'm Jada." She shook his hand softly.

"It's nice to meet you, Jada." He cleared his throat awkwardly. "Can I say that I find you delicious?" His gaze did not waver from her eyes.

Jada flinched under his gaze. His comment had also surprised her. She'd never been called delicious; she didn't know if she should be worried enough to cuff her pepper spray in her hand or blush under such a sensual description. "Delicious, huh? Should I be worried?"

"You know, you probably should be but not the kind of worried that has you squeezing your pepper spray right now." He nodded towards her hand. "But the kind that tells you a man finds you extremely attractive enough to completely embarrass himself by calling you delicious." His laugh was deep, as if it had crawled out of his belly and forced its way out of his mouth. "Wow. I can't believe I said that." He scratched his temple. "You can partially count it to my hunger, but make no mistake, when I saw you, your full figure, curves in the best places. And then, once you turned, looking at me with those almond shaped, dark eyes, and that little nose, I'm sorry, but I found you to look absolutely delicious. You're stunning." He placed his hands in his pocket and rocked back and forth on the heels of his shoes.

"Wow. That is the longest come-on I've ever heard. But thank you." She batted her eyes slowly. "It's certainly not every day that a girl is flattered in such a way."

"I'm glad I could be of help. Are you here with anyone?" He looked around the room, surveying the crowd.

"No well--umm--yes, I'm here with a friend for Spring Break."

He held up his hands in protest. "Whoa! Clarification needed. Are you a student or a teacher?" He seemed to be genuinely afraid of her answer.

"Teacher." She smiled back at him, adjusting the tote strap on her shoulder.

He fanned his hand across his chest. "Oh, God. Good." He released a long breath.

"What if I had been a student?" She inquired, raising her eyebrow.

"I would've just walked away."

"Hmph. Nowadays that's good to hear," she scoffed.

"Whoa. I sense a story behind that comment."

"Oh, you have no idea."

"But I'd like to. Over dinner. Are you free tonight?"

She was, but Jada couldn't bring herself to agree to it. Thoughts of Caleb flashed in her mind. "How long are you in town?" She asked, her question surprising both him and her. "And how do I know that *you* aren't a student?"

He chuckled softly. "I'm here until the end of the week for an art exhibit, and clearly, my corny come-on should tell you that I am far removed from being a scholar."

Jada smiled, shifting her weight from one foot to the other. "I can't go to dinner tonight, but how about tomorrow?"

A grin slid across his lips. "I look forward to it." He pulled his phone out of his pocket and held it out towards her. "Do you mind putting your number in my phone?"

"Sure." Jada quickly typed her number in the contacts and handed it back to him before giving a small wave and smile and joining Lena at the door.

Lena gave her a knowing smile, clutching her arm. "Girrrl, who was that? Brotha' was fine." She looked back in Johnathan's direction dramatically. He offered a salute.

Jada slapped her hand before dragging her down the sidewalk. She looked back cautiously before speaking. "Did you see all that chocolate?"

"Yes, ma'am. I'm scared of you." Her friend pinched her wrist. "Your confused behind would be the one to find a Spring Break fling while my single behind lusting after art."

Jada howled. "Stop it. I'm not confused, and I've been telling you to look up from the canvas every now and then."

"Girl, if you would've told me that I was missing Mr. Chocolate, I'd never hang my head and paint again. So, what are you going to do because Jada, girl, I think you're playing with fire." She linked her arm in Jada's.

Jada loosened her grip and pulled her shades down. "What fire? Technically, I'm single."

"Yeah, *technically* single, but be real. You're still holding out for Caleb." She signaled for a taxi. "Are you sure about getting involved with this guy before you've really moved on from another?" They stepped back as a taxi pulled next to the curb.

Jada slid onto the backseat first. "Dang, Lena, you act like I'm getting ready to marry the man. Caleb and I haven't spoken. He's not ready, and I'm not waiting for him anymore. Why not explore my options?"

"How about because you might end up liking this guy?" She stared back at Jada, which Jada found unsettling being that she couldn't see her eyes behind the shades.

"Is it such a crime if I end up liking him?"

"No, I think you deserve some fun, but that guy doesn't seem like the let's-hang-for-one-night-kind-of-guy. Are you ready for that?"

"I--" Jada exhaled loudly and peered out of the window at the large arch that punctured the Missouri sky. She didn't have an answer. She wasn't sure if she was ready to date or not, but there was only one way to find out.

***

That night, she'd considered calling Caleb back, just to get verification that she should move on, but her finger hovered over the call button. She'd drifted off to sleep, her phone mere inches from her hand, but her dreams were clouded with thoughts of Johnathan.

Now, looking down at his good morning text, she was reminded of the night they'd shared over fondue, baked potatoes, and steaks. The conversation had flowed so smoothly that it unnerved her to think that they had just met for the first time. They had discussed their families, hobbies, and goals, and she had been elated to find that they had so much in common. He'd made it his business to open every single door for her, to walk her into her hotel lobby to ensure her safety; he'd even allowed her to take a picture of him to send to her mother as a safety precaution. As the night ended, he'd wrapped her in a warm and tight embrace, the stubble along his jaw, scratching Jada's cheek, a feeling she didn't know she missed. His masculine scent floated into her nostrils, and she released him hesitantly, as he pecked her softly on the cheek and promised to call her the next morning.

He'd kept his promise and called, and for the next few days, whenever she wasn't out shopping and primping with Lena, she was gallivanting around the city with him.

They'd spoken every day since her return home. She wasn't one to do long distance relationships, especially with him being six hours away in Atlanta, but she had made a personal vow not to immediately jump to conclusions and worry endlessly about another man and his commitment to her and a future. It was much too soon to start wondering about a relationship, and if a man didn't see her worth, she was no longer allowing him to string her along. She typed a quick good morning and smiley face back to him before slipping her phone back into her pocket.

The school was awfully quiet. She figured that everyone was exhausted from their one-week excursions, but she didn't even smell Ms. Allen's routine coffee brew in the air. She peeped around the corner and into the teacher's lounge; it was dark. That was odd. Usually, Ms. Allen always brewed coffee and provided some form of breakfast pastry for the faculty. Teachers would chatter loudly as they entered the lounge, some accidentally spilling coffee on their shirts while catching up on the latest school gossip.

Jada continued to her classroom, her heels clicking a rhythm down the freshly-waxed floor. Mr. Oliver tipped his hat in her direction and moseyed into his tiny little room. After entering the room, Jada erased her boards and wrote the objective and bell ringer for the day followed by the vocabulary word of the day. She began straightening up the papers on her desk, running across the letter of intent that was past due. Before Spring Break, Mr. Jackson had asked the faculty to complete letters of intent, indicating their intention to return to the school the following year. She signed the paper and walked quickly to Mr. Jackson's office. Ms. Allen, the secretary, stood and said her name just as Jada knocked on his door.

The door creaked open, revealing the office's bareness. All of his plaques and certificates of achievement were gone. The desk sparkled as if it had just been cleaned, and the lines in the carpet seemed fresh as though it had been vacuumed recently.

Jada turned, her mouth hanging open and her eyes asking Ms. Allen for answers. The woman shrugged her shoulders before turning her attention to the ringing phone.

Jada marched out of the office and down the hall to Mr. Dennis, the Assistant Principal's office. The door was wide open, but it, too, had been wiped clean. She stepped in and flipped the light switch. The only thing left on the desk was a worn ticket to the Giggle's Comedy House. Jada picked up the ticket, remembering when Mr. Dennis had called her to his office only to ask her if she wanted to go to a comedy show with him. She'd been quick to remind him that he was married, to which he'd responded by reassuring her that it was strictly a platonic offer. She'd refused, but his eyes had continuously exuded lust, and she had made it a point not to visit his office again.

Now, other than the flimsy ticket stub, there were no signs of him having ever been there. Just then, Mr. Rucker, the other assistant principal, walked past the office. Jada threw the ticket on the desk and ran after him.

He turned when she called his name. His face drooped from what appeared to be lack of sleep, and his usually bright, blue eyes were dim and dark. His hair was ruffled atop his head, and his clothes seemed to be thrown on him, nonchalantly. Jada hesitated to ask him about the two principals.

"Umm, I went to visit Mr. Jackson, and all of his belongings are gone." She pointed towards the front office; her eyes pleaded with him for answers.

He ran his hand through his hair, making himself appear more disheveled. "I'm going to call a meeting with everyone at the close of the school day. We'll explain everything then."

Jada was displeased with his answer, and she was sure that it was evident in her face. She dragged herself to the classroom, speculating on what could have happened. The bell rang, and the students ran into the school, their tongues wagging non-stop about their Spring Break.

Chapter Fourteen

All day, Jada seemed to be going through the motions. Her head was not in the classroom. She couldn't help but feel that something wasn't right.

Ms. Allen's voice sounded on the intercom. "Ms. Harris, can you please come to the office for a minute?"

Her breath caught in her throat. "S-sure."

Her fourth period students looked back at her puzzled. There was a slight tap on her door, and Coach Quinn, the new basketball coach, informed her that he was there to watch her class while she was away. She walked to the office slowly, mulling over all of the possibilities. She pushed open the office door to Ms. Allen, who gestured for her to go into the conference room.

Two men, one black and one white, both in white collar shirts and khaki pants greeted her. Shortly after, a woman with long blonde hair and bright red lipstick entered the room and settled in a chair between the two. The white guy with the curly brown hair spoke first.

"Ms. Harris, we work in the Human Resources Department for the school. We want to ask you a few questions about the work environment here."

Jada nodded sternly. "Okay."

"How would you describe your time here at Caldwin High?" Their pens hovered above their clipboards, their badges hanging from their shirts.

"Well, it's been a learning experience."

"In what way?" The black guy asked.

"Well, I started teaching college first, so it has taken some getting used to. You know, with the kids and their huge personalities and their parents, but Mr. Jackson was very helpful."

Their pens squiggled noisily against along the paper. "And how would you describe your relationship with Mr. Jackson?"

Jada arched her eyebrow in confusion. "What do you mean?"

The pale-skinned woman piped in. "Was it strictly professional, more personal, et cetera, et cetera?" she asked dryly.

"It was professional. He was always very cordial and patient with me as a first-year teacher."

"Have the two of you every exchanged text messages?"

"No, well, yes, when I had to call in sick one day."

"Would you be willing to show us these messages on your phone?"

"Y-yes. Can you tell me what's going on?" She tucked her hair behind her ear nervously before fumbling with her fingers in her lap.

"We will, but we have a few more questions for you first." The woman spoke firmly, her teeth stained with red lipstick. "Can you tell us about your relationship with the Assistant Principal, Mr. Dennis?"

"Ummm. Well, I kept it professional. There were times that I felt he wanted it to be more personal."

Curly hair spoke up. "Can you tell us about those times?"

Jada fidgeted in her seat, crossing her ankles. "Well, one time he invited me to a comedy show, but I turned him down."

"Did he indicate that it would be anything more than a platonic outing?" the woman asked.

"He said it would be platonic, but the way he stared at me said something different."

"Okay. Are you aware that both Mr. Jackson and Mr. Dennis are married?"

Jada nodded her head. "I've never met Mr. Dennis' wife, but I saw pictures in his office. I met Mr. Jackson's wife at a basketball game."

"Okay, good. Last question, have you ever noticed any inappropriate behavior between the two principals and other co-workers?"

Jada struggled to recall a time when she'd witnessed such an instance. "No, I didn't. Look, I don't know what's going on, but Mr. Jackson is a great principal for this school. The students respect h---"

"Both principals have been reported for sexual harassment and inappropriately touching employees." The blonde cut her off. "We're here to investigate and determine the severity of the accusations." The woman rested the pen on her bottom lip.

Jada couldn't speak. She could believe the accusations when it came to Mr. Dennis, but there was no way that Mr. Jackson had intentionally harassed anyone. She replayed the faculty meetings in her head. Nothing came to mind. "I'm sorry but Mr. Jackson wouldn't do that. He has always been professional."

"Thank you for coming, Ms. Harris." Curly-hair stood and extended his hand. "We hope to see you at the faculty meeting this afternoon." He walked over and opened the door.

As Jada walked towards the door, Ms. Henson, the guidance counselor, passed her slowly, her eyes fastened to the ground and her shoulders sagging heavily. Jada hadn't seen very much of her since their conversation at the beginning of the semester in the teachers' lounge, and on rare occasions when she did see her, she'd been in good spirits, nearly skipping to her office. Jada offered her a small reassuring smile, but the woman quickly shifted her eyes back to the floor.

"Thanks for coming, Ms. Henson." Curly greeted, ushering her into the room.

***

The news of the two principals being suspended spread rapidly around the school. The students babbled uncontrollably throughout the day. From them, Jada had learned that two teachers had accused the principals of making unwarranted sexual advances, which had resulted in their temporary suspensions. She wasn't sure how accurate the rumors were, but it wouldn't be the first time that they would prove to be more in-the-know than most of the teachers in the school. For Mr. Jackson's sake, she prayed that they were wrong.

The teacher's lounge was full of teachers during lunch. Jada couldn't remember a time when she had ever seen the lounge so busy. She settled in a chair across from Mrs. Inglewood, who sat quietly peeling an orange. She whispered across the table to Jada.

173

"Did they interview you, too?"

Jada nodded, pulling a sandwich, potato chips, and a bottle of water from her lunch bag. "I think you meant to ask if they grilled me."

"Oh, honey, me too.

Jada pulled the plastic wrap from her sandwich. "And the kids are talking non-stop about it. It's ridiculous."

"Oh, baby. You ain't got to tell me." She whispered loudly. "Supposedly," She looked around to see who was listening. "Mr. Williams and Mr. Flemings, the U.S. government teacher, wrote letters to the Human Resources Department."

"Letters?" Jada whispered back. "What did they say?"

"I'm not exactly sure, but I heard that one of them said something about walking in and seeing Mr. Dennis fondling one of the teacher's butts, and the other letter was about Mr. Jackson having sex with a teacher while on campus."

"No way." Jada mouthed, leaning forward onto the table.

Mrs. Inglewood stabbed the lettuce drizzled in ranch on her plate, plopping it in her mouth. "Yep. Right now, I don't know which teachers, but it won't be long before the rumor mill gets to turning. Just get ready."

Jada shook her head and stuffed her mouth with the rest of her sandwich. The lunch bell sounded loudly. She and Mrs. Inglewood grabbed their lunch boxes and shuffled out of the lounge.

***

"Good Afternoon, all!" The blonde with the HR badge, the tight black dress, and red lipstick spoke sternly as she stood in front of the distracted, rambunctious group. "I'm glad that you all could make it. We will not be before you long. As most of you know, we are here on behalf of the Human Resource Department." She crossed her arms tightly over her breasts, piercing her lips together in a sour pucker. She paced slowly back and forth in front of the librarian's desk, appearing to be selecting her next words carefully.

The group quieted. Everyone seemed to be on the edge of their seats waiting for her to deliver what they all thought would be bad news. Jada sat on her hands, rocking and watching, impatiently waiting. Everyone had been whispering in corners throughout the school day. They seemed to be sizing each other up, trying to pinpoint the two teachers who had come forward. Jada found that whispers ceased when she rounded corners or entered a room; she knew that most of the teachers expected her to be one of the culprits.

The blonde continued. "Unfortunately, Mr. Jackson and Mr. Dennis will not be returning due to sexual harassment claims." Tongues began to wag. "Now, now," She patted the air. "We don't want to make a huge spectacle of this situation. We don't want it plastered all on the news. So, we're asking that you keep this discussion confidential."

Jada snorted, crossing her arms over her chest. By tomorrow morning, everyone in the school would know. She could guess that the students would sniff out the accusers easily.

"Our goal here at Caldwin High is to ensure that all employees feel safe and protected at all times. We appreciate you all for being here, so you can be sure that if you ever feel threatened or pressured, we will do everything we can to alleviate it. We know that it's not easy to work with these students, but we also know that you chose to be teachers to change lives. That's what we want the focus in this building to be on."

Mrs. Kimble shifted in her seat, massaging her neck softly. Jada assumed that she was deeply affected by Mr. Jackson's removal from the school, especially being that they were so close, and he always called on her to help with large projects and school events. Together, Jada had come to see them as a power team. She shot Mrs. Kimble a reassuring smile. She nodded in acknowledgement before darting her eyes at Coach Lewis, who was leaning against the wall, his large arms crossed tightly over his chest, staring back at her intensely.

Jada could feel the electricity that bounced between them. She didn't know if it was sexual chemistry or anger, but it was clear that they had words for each other.

"For the remainder of the school year, Mr. Rucker will serve as the principal." Chatter sounded around the room. "We're confident that he will be able to step in and serve you all in the best way possible. Once again, we ask that you refrain from discussing this meeting with students and others outside of this room. Mr. Rucker, do you have any words?"

He grinned uncomfortably, shaking his head. The blonde turned back the group. "Meeting adjourned."

People filed slowly out of the room. "Girl, this is a mess. Aint it?" Mr. Williams came up and grabbed her elbow, slowly steering her out of the library.

"Yeah, it really is. It's just too much."

"Wouldn't be if folks learned to keep their hands to themselves." His vengeful tone caught Jada off guard.

"You speak as if you know for a fact that they did it." She stopped to face him.

He looked about them quickly before grabbing her arm and pulling her towards his classroom. After the closing the door behind them, he slowly pulled his glasses from his face. "Look, Ima tell you this, but it's between me and you. Okay?"

Jada nodded, staring back into his small, dark eyes.

"I wrote one of the letters to the superintendent." He fell into the rolling chair positioned behind his desk, dropping his glasses onto the wooden desk, and running his hand through his budding, unruly kinky curls.

"But why?" Jada slid into the small desk, leaning forward on her elbows. "Why would you do that? Why lie?"

"I didn't lie. I walked in on Mr. Dennis feeling Ms. Henson up. I mean, groping her breasts like a newborn baby."

"Ms. Henson the guidance counselor?"

"Now you know it ain't no other Ms. Henson working here." He stared back at her sarcastically. "He had no business touching her. He's a married man, and then, when I talked to her afterwards, she made it clear that he had pretty much pressured her into it, threatening her job and stuff. She been sleeping with him since before Christmas break." His faced was framed in sadness.

Jada's mouth was dry. She thought back to her conversation with Ms. Henson on her first day. Ms. Henson's words echoed in her mind. *Sometimes you have to get 'em however you can.* She knew that Mr. Williams had been misinformed. She couldn't understand why Ms. Henson would lie to one of her closest friends in the school, and clearly, it was weighing heavily on him. Jada made a mental note to speak with her about it.

***

"I don't know what you mean." The guidance counselor stared back at her, a bored expression on her face.

"You know exactly what I mean. You told Mr. Williams that Mr. Daniels forced you into having an affair with him. But I distinctly remember you telling me when I first got here that you would be open to having any man, even a married one. You lied on him!" Jada tapped the desk nestled between them, rising from the seat.

"Look, it's no surprise to anyone that he was caught with his pants down. Everyone knew that he had a wandering eye." She turned quickly and began typing on the computer keyboard.

Jada walked around to stand in front of her. "So, that's still not okay. You can't falsely accuse him just because people will believe it!" She yanked the monitor cord from the outlet, causing the computer screen to black out. The woman looked up suddenly. Jada wasn't sure when the tears developed in the corner of her eyes, but they began to flow.

179

"Mr. Williams knows the truth, but what was I supposed to do? Have everyone think of me as some floozy?! S-s-s-some sidepiece?!" She yanked a tissue from the Kleenex box at the corner of her desk and blew hard. I didn't expect Mr. Williams to walk in, and I was just so embarrassed. You don't know what it's like being me. I haven't had a man show me that kind of attention in years, since my daughter was born! H-h-he made me promises, and as soon as Mr. Williams walked in, he stopped responding to my text, blocked my calls, and was never available to meet with me. All his promises evaporated," she spat. "If he wasn't ignoring me, he was treating my like every other teacher in this school."

Jada knew she was looking at a woman scorned, one absolutely furious with her unfortunate circumstances. She spoke softly, "You lied to save face?"

"Come on, Mr. Williams is as gay as the tape dispenser on his desk. I knew he wouldn't be able to keep it a secret, so I went to him and told him Mr. Dennis was harassing me. I need this job, and I can't afford to start over. He decided to write the letter to the superintendent, and I just co-signed."

"But you said he knew the truth." Jada cocked her head sideways, amazed by what she was hearing.

"He didn't at first, until he had to use my computer and ran across an email with a picture of Mr. Dennis in a rather vulnerable position. But as it turns out, he didn't like many of Mr. Dennis' snide comments about gay people either. So, it was a win-win." She peeked at Jada through lowered eyelashes and smeared eyeliner. "Look, I didn't expect him to write the letter, but once he did, I had to protect myself."

Jada plopped down into the small, burgundy chair. She hadn't liked Mr. Dennis either, but she wouldn't have wished such an ordeal on him. Looking at Ms. Henson now, it seemed as though her shoulders sagged less, and the color seemed to be returning to her light-skin cheeks. Jada realized that she was looking at a woman with years of deep-seated hurt and betrayal. Her eyelids were sunken in and dark from sleep deprivation, and her fiery red hair was pulled up into a high puff on top of her head. Sitting behind the large desk, she looked small and child-like. Her demeanor saddened Jada, and even though she knew that she should go and tell someone what really happened, she knew that she wouldn't. For once, she wanted Ms. Henson to feel that she had won, plus she wasn't sure that it would do anything but cause the counselor and Mr. Williams to lose their jobs, that's if anyone even believed her. She wasn't sure that it was worth the trouble.

"I don't agree with what you did, but tell me, did Mr. Williams write the letter about Mr. Jackson, too?"

"Oh, no. That was all Mr. Flemings, the U.S. Government teacher. He caught Mrs. Kimble and Mr. Jackson in the fieldhouse together."

Jada inhaled sharply. "But wait, I thought---."

"What?" The counselor leaned forward. "You thought Mrs. Kimble was only sleeping with Coach Lewis?"

Her eyes widened. "You knew?"

"Psssh, please. Everyone knew. They've been meeting up in that fieldhouse for years. Just no one's said anything. Coach Lewis has a reputation around here, and now, she does, too."

"Wow," Jada mouthed. "I would have never guessed that she and Mr. Jackson. Oh, my God." She cupped her face in her hand. "But if Mr. Fleming caught them together, why is she still here?"

"Well, I heard that she told HR that she felt pressured because he was the principal." She shrugged, wiping the eyeliner from her lash line.

"But they don't know that it was consensual or about Coach Lewis?"

"Right. These are grown folks. You let them take care of their own stuff. Plus, if you look up Mr. Jackson, you'll see that he had been fired at his first school for something similar. You can't help these folks. They here for themselves."

Jada felt uneasy with the hypocritical nature of her words. Now, Jada viewed Mr. Jackson's relationship with and reliance on Mrs. Kimble differently. It made more sense. She was even more enraged by her naivety in believing Mrs. Kimble's sob story about her husband and their marriage. It unnerved her even more to know that in his own way, Coach Lewis had been more honest than everyone she'd encountered so far.

She stood and walked towards the door. She could feel the counselor's questioning eyes on the back of her head. She halted at the door. "No, I'm not going to say anything, but I expected so much more from you," she said softly, never looking back. She passed Mr. Williams, who gave her a knowing glance before rushing into the office. She was disappointed in all of them, especially Mr. Jackson.

"You can't give people the benefit of the doubt in this profession, Ms. Harris," a smiling Ms. Calloway stated, walking towards her. "They'll disappoint you every time." She brushed past Jada, entering the counselor's office and slamming the door.

Jada jumped at the sound. Walking past each person in the hall, she found herself questioning everyone and his or her intentions, attempting to peer into their souls for something, anything, she'd missed before. To say that she felt as though she was losing her mind was an understatement. She just couldn't believe anything they said about Mr. Jackson. Yes, he and Mrs. Kimble were relatively close, but other than completing many tasks together, he had never shown anything outside of professional interest in the woman. And Jada knew about Mrs. Kimble's promiscuous escapades with Coach Lewis; there was no way that Mr. Jackson would be willing to sacrifice his position for a quick romp with a woman like her. On top of that, his wife was absolutely stunning. Jada shook her conversation with Ms. Henson out of her head. She wasn't sure what to think anymore, but one thing was for sure: if Ms. Henson would lie about her own sexual exploits, there was no doubt that she'd lie about others.

***

Jada yanked the gear back into park and leaned closer to the rearview mirror as she watched Mrs. Kimble sashay up to the wooden fieldhouse door, looking around before making four rapid taps and entering quickly. Jada looked around to see if anyone else was watching. The parking lot was silent and practically empty. Still, considering that it was close to dinnertime, she was surprised to see Mrs. Kimble still on campus. She sat and pondered on what she should do, her nails tapping against the steering wheel. She could take Mrs. Kimble's word or she could go see if----well--- she didn't know what else she could expect. Other than Mrs. Kimble's consistent visits to the fieldhouse with Coach Lewis after school hours, Jada had no other reason not to trust her. Yet, Jada found herself exiting her car, gently closing the door, and tiptoeing up to the door. Her chest heaved up and down as she pressed her ear against the door. She could hear scuffles against the floor and muffled noises, and then, it was quiet. Jada pressed her body closer to the door, but there was nothing. She pulled away abruptly, her eyes searching the parking lot. She reached for her phone but realized she'd left it in the car. A loud, guttural moan from behind the door startled her, and she pulled the door handle.

The room was dark, with the only stream of light coming from the windows on each wall. Jada's eyes searched the darkness as low moans and heavy breathing permeated the air. Movement on one of the weight benches caught her attention. The half-naked bodies seemed to be entangled, glistening in perspiration, and the hands clawed at skin as if desperate. Jada stood watching as if frozen as the man's hands slowly traveled up the woman's long leg, which he placed on his shoulder just before Mrs. Kimble released a shrill cry. His head fell back and a husky growl escaped from his lips and shook the walls, and Jada saw it. She saw him. Mr. Jackson's dark brown skin seemed to melt into the woman's body as he quivered against her, releasing her leg and exhaling loudly.

He chuckled before saying, "Now that, *that's* worth losing a job for." He planted a sloppy kiss on her lips and slapped her thigh. "Come here, woman." He lifted her from the bench, and sat down heavily with her legs fastened securely around his waist. Mrs. Kimble's eyes met Jada's in a challenging and facetious stare. She began to moan loudly with the soft and sultry kisses he placed along her collarbone. She smiled at Jada in triumph.

"Baby," she breathed between moans. "What are we gonna do?"

He slowly pulled his head up from her exposed breast. "Well, I'll find another job the same way I found this one. The school is not going to want the public to know about all this, so I'm not worried about any of this following me. And you," He caressed her thigh and captured her lips in a rough kiss. "You will hold it down here for, daddy, okay?"

She wiggled on his lap, pulling her eyes away from Jada to gaze back at him. "Whatever you say." She smiled at him.

"Good. You practically run the school anyway. As long as we keep a low profile, we'll be good. Neither one of us needs a messy divorce or people all in our business. We got a good thing going." His attention returned to her breast. She looked to the door expectantly, but Jada was gone.

Jada walked to her car as if in a trance. It wasn't for a lack of belief that she walked slowly, but rather how incorrect she'd been about so much that seemed to stun her into silence and trance-like movement as she drove home. It was the lack of words she had as she watched the two canoodle, the surprise at how quickly her own words of support and repudiation had turned on her, and the open defiance of and disregard for leadership positions and responsibilities that resonated in her mind. She chided herself on being fairly upright and confrontational when necessary; yet, she currently had nothing for this situation, no words, no solutions, just nothing. For the first time, she understood why Caleb had developed such a passive and neutral approach to people. He was protecting himself, always assessing everyone at face-value rather than based on their titles or positions, and for the first time since the news broke about Vanessa and Coach Young, she wished she had done the same thing.

Her mother's words echoed in her mind: *When people show you who they really are, baby, you better believe them.* And boy did she believe them now.

Chapter Fifteen

"Dang, I thought they were playin', but they really did get Mr. Jackson's ole wearing-grandma's-bingo-bright-pants-to-school-looking self! It's been almost two weeks now!" Ashton howled, walking into the classroom.

"Sho' did cuz! Now, who ima check??" Ashton and DeQuan slapped hands, laughing.

"Guys, you're too loud." Jada warned, sensing a headache.

They scurried to their desks and began working on their bell ringer assignment. Just then, Jada's phone vibrated in the pocket of her leopard print cardigan. There was a message from Caleb:

Hey, I know you're probably busy but want you to know you're on my mind..... Miss you.

Even though part of her wanted to talk to him about everything, she still hadn't responded to any of his messages. He still hadn't sent her the message that she was looking for, and she knew it was their history that made her want to talk to him, not a future. She deleted his message and typed a quick good morning to Johnathan. They'd grown closer and closer every day. Even though they both worked throughout most of the day, he still made time for her every night. She had become accustomed to their conversations before bed. He surprised her often, either with a romance novel from Rochelle Alers, her favorite author, waiting on her doorstep or the personal things he revealed about himself at the most unexpected times. They were already scheduling a time for him to come visit her from Atlanta, and she was looking forward to it, especially after venting to him about everything happening in the school.

Since that day with Ms. Henson, she'd purposely stayed clear of her, Mr. Williams, and Ms. Calloway. However, it seemed that the ordeal had only brought them closer. She rarely saw one without the others. They ceased talking whenever she entered the room and cut their eyes at her whenever she spoke in the faculty meetings. Unlike Ms. Calloway, however, the other two were always trying to butter up to her when alone. It always ended the same way, with Jada having very little to say to them both. And she definitely had nothing to say to Mrs. Kimble. Instead, Jada had thrown herself deeper into her work, spending more time with her family to keep a clear head, especially with Mr. Rucker in charge now.

Things had certainly changed. Many of the white teachers were more in charge now that both of the black leaders had been removed, and Mr. Rucker's easy-going, goofy persona had changed just as fast. He'd become overbearing, even irate at times when he didn't feel the staff was taking him serious. At one point, he'd even cursed out one of the lunch ladies for not delivering his lunch to his office on time. Unfortunately, his new personality didn't faze most people, not even the students, and Jada could see his willpower slipping away from him with each passing day. She sympathized with him but knew that there was no way that she could help him.

She passed the graphic organizers out to the students. "Okay, so now, I want you all to compare Romeo and Juliet's feelings for each other. Let's see who you all think cares the most."

"Oh, Juliet definitely cares more!" Demetria yelled.

Jada was taken aback by her quick response. "Demetria, why do you say that?"

"Because that's the way it is. Women always care more than men." Others murmured their agreement.

"Why do you think that is?"

"It's just the way we were wired. Like, even with black and white people. I think black people are more likely to care about all people, but most white folks only care about themselves."

"That's not true," interjected Sara, a white girl who had recently joined the class. "I'm white but I like hanging out with black people more than white people."

"Yeah. Right now you do, but wait. All that will change." Demetria frowned at the girl.

"Okay, okay, ladies. Clearly, you both have ideas when it relates to race. What I heard is that some of you believe that your background can influence how you love and treat people. Can we agree on that?"

Both girls pondered, exchanging glances, before nodding their heads in agreement.

"Cool. Now, I'd like for you to make an assertion about Romeo's love for Juliet, and in the boxes, you're going to write down evidence from the play along with the page number. What do we use as evidence for our assertions?"

"Quotes!!" They all yelled loudly.

She beamed. "Good. Now, once you finish with Romeo, do the same thing for Juliet."

Ashton raised his hand. "Ms. H., do I have to start with Romeo?"

"No, Ashton, you can start with Julie--"

"Ms. Harris?" The intercom in the classroom boomed with Ms. Allen's raspy voice.

"Yes?"

"Can you please send Ashton Gross to the office with his belongings?"

"He's on his way."

A round of "Oooooo's" echoed around the room. The boy snatched up his bag and strolled out of the room. Jada prayed that he wasn't in trouble. Once she'd spoken to Mr. Jackson about him, he didn't seem to have any more trouble, but now that Mr. Jackson was gone, she hoped Mrs. Barnes wasn't up to her old tricks.

"Okay, ladies and gentlemen, let's get back to work!" She offered a quick prayer up to God, before strolling around the room, helping each student as needed.

***

The school dismissal bell rang loudly. Jada stacked the ungraded papers on top of each other, her hands already aching from all of the grading she had to do.

"Hey, Ms. Harris!" Jose, a student from her first period class yelled, leaning into the classroom.

"Hey, Jose!" She yelled back.

"You heard about Ashton?" His face suddenly turned solemn. She ceased stacking the papers.

"What about Ashton?"

"He's been expelled. They say he'll have to repeat 9th grade."

Jada felt the wind knocked out of her stomach. "But why?"

"He cursed out Mrs. Barnes this morning before first period." This news surprised Jada, even more that she was just hearing about it. She was sure that Jose had the story wrong. There was no way that the punishment fit the crime. Kids cursed out teachers every day here. She hadn't heard of anyone getting more than a week's suspension.

"Thanks for telling me Jose."

"Welcome." The boy gave a small smile before running down the opposite end of the hall, calling after his friends.

Jada was fuming. Stuffing the papers into her work bag, she locked the classroom door and marched to Mr. Rucker's office. She tapped heavily on the open door before stepping into the room without invitation. He looked up quickly, annoyance flashed in his eyes.

"How can I help you, Ms. Harris?"

"I would like to know what happened to Ashton Gross." She sat in the chair adjacent to his desk, which seemed to annoy him more.

"Ah, Mr. Gross was expelled."

"I know that. I would like to know why."

"He cursed out Mrs. Barnes."

"I know that, too. Isn't expulsion too harsh for such a thing? He didn't touch her."

"Ms. Harris, we cannot excuse his behavior. Plus, he and Mrs. Barnes have had several conflicts in the past."

She leaned forward in the chair, slapping the desk with her bare hand. "Don't you find it odd that she is the only teacher that writes him up? And after every infraction, especially those as minor as his, shouldn't he come back with a clean slate? He doesn't bother anyone. He doesn't get into fights, no record or anything."

"Look, Ms. Harris. I made the best decision I could. His parents didn't put up a fight. Why are you?"

"Because they don't know how!" she yelled. "If you believe this is fair, you can't possibly be the leader I thought you were. If you keep a boy like Ashton out of school until next year, God knows what will happen, Mr. Rucker."

"You're being slightly dramatic, don't you think? Even Mrs. Calloway agreed with my decision. I'm sorry, but we gave Mr. Gross several opportunities to fall in line."

"Fall in line?" Jada scoffed. "This is amazing," She said absentmindedly.

"Is that all, Ms. Harris?" Mr. Rucker asked impatiently, the rolls of his chin jiggling as he spoke.

She yanked her bag off the floor and stomped out of the office, stopping in the teacher's lounge to dial Ashton's home. His mother answered the phone roughly.

"Hello, Mrs. Gross. I am Ms. Harris, Ashton's English teacher at Caldwin."

"Yeah?" The woman sounded agitated.

"I hope I didn't catch you at a bad time, but I just heard about Ashton's expulsion. I understand that you might be ang--"

"Look, baby" the woman interrupted. "Thanks for calling, but I gotta get ready for work."

Jada pulled the phone from her ear and stared at the mouthpiece. "I-I understand, but I thought you might not be very happy about Ashton being expelled."

"Every child has been expelled once or twice before. It ain't nothin' he won't be able to get through."

"I understand, ma'am, but I don't agree with him being expelled. I--."

"Look, I appreciate ya callin' but Ashton fine. We already got him lookin' fo' a job to bring some extra money in tha' house."

Jada inhaled sharply, not sure what to do with what she was hearing. "A-a job ma'am? But Ashton is too smart to just be working."

"Look here, lady. You must gone give us some extra money? You don't think I'm smart because I work. I know you got yo' fancy degrees and all, but some of us gotta get money doing some real work. Now, I'm fixin' to get ready for work."

"Ma'am, that's not at all what I meant. I---" The dial tone screamed in her ear. She placed the phone back on the receiver, tossing the options around in her head. She could go to the school board, but without the support from his family, she doubted it would do any good. She had assumed that his parents would be fuming as she was, ready to fight back and demand another punishment in place of his expulsion, but instead, she'd ended up feeling as though she'd been punched in the stomach. She knew that a student like Ashton would be beating himself up every day, and the fact that he would have to come back as a repeating 9th grader was just another blow. She had to do something. She headed towards Coach Lewis's classroom. Mrs. Kimble sat perched up on the corner of his desk. She slowly slid off the desk when she noticed Jada standing in the door.

"I'll see you later, Coach." She pranced past Jada, smirking as she reached the door. Jada grunted and rolled her eyes.

"What's going on, Ms. H?" Coach Lewis crossed his legs at the ankle.

"It's Harris, but I might need your help."

He appeared shocked. "You? Need *my* help? Oh, this must be big."

"It's Ashton Gross. I know he plays for you, and he was expelled today."

"Yeah. What's the problem?" He seemed genuinely confused.

"What do you mean 'what's the problem'? He shouldn't have been expelled!"

"Says who?"

"What do you mean? Says me. You should, too! Don't you think it's too harsh of a punishment? He's not a bad kid." She stepped closer, looking for any inkling that her words resonated with him. She found none.

"Look, stuff like this happens all the time. He cursed out his teacher. There are consequences."

"I understand that there are consequences, but the punishment doesn't fit the crime."

"It does when you're a little black boy that curses out a white woman, who has written you up several times. Right now, it's a matter of paper trail, and she has that." He sat up and gathered a stack of papers in the corner of his desk.

"How can you say that as if it is okay?" She gawked at him, not believing her ears.

"Look, it's been okay for years. The school board is made up of all white folks and one brotha', and on top of that, I bet you called his parents."

Her back straightened at his words.

"Let me guess, they didn't sound the least bit concerned." She remained silent. He shook his head and leaned forward in the chair, nestling his hands under his chin. "Let it go, Harris. Without his parents, there is certainly nothing you can do."

Tears gathered in her eyes at the truth behind his words. It stung. She blinked several times. "But he plays for you. He shows up for practice religiously. I hear him talking about plays and being a football player and stuff. Don't you feel something for him or want to do something?"

"Sure, I do." He leaned back in the chair. "But I also know my role. I'm a football coach. I'm not his parents, the superintendent, Superman, and I sure as heck ain't Jesus. I can't save every boy that decides to curse out little Miss White Woman. I play my role. Harris, you gotta start playing yours. You can't save 'em all."

She turned and walked swiftly to her car with the tears cascading down her chubby cheeks as the engine roared to life. She felt the mountain building in her throat and attempted to swallow it, but it pushed, its peak coming out in the form of a loud sob that rippled through her body. She sat in the parking lot, for the next thirty minutes, wailing mostly out of regret that she hadn't done more sooner and then out of mere disappointment in the system that had just thrown a young, vibrant, idle boy on the street and that made his parents believe it was okay. She wept in wild abandonment for them.

Chapter Sixteen

He smelled like a bark of slow-burning Mahogany wood freshly coated in raindrops. Jada inhaled slowly, lingering in his scent and his arms for longer than she knew she probably should, but looking up into his eyes, she saw more peace than she had experienced in the past week. She could feel his toned, muscular body against her plump form. Her hands rested on his pecks, his heart pounding under her palm. She smiled up at his sculpted face, his hair freshly cut and lined, smooth, dark, and wavy. His low-cut beard smelled of pine and cocoa butter, and she relished in the way her body responded to his. She clung to him tighter, her shoulders drooping as he planted a sultry kiss on her forehead, kneading her back slowly and sensually. Jada was surprised by the deep guttural moan that escaped from her parted lips. He chuckled softly, his chest vibrating against her cheek.

"Sorry." She snickered, pulling away from him slowly.

"No apology necessary. The feeling is mutual. Come here." Johnathan pulled her back into a long embrace. "I've been wanting to hold you like this again since we left each other in March. My only regret is that this weekend isn't long enough." He sighed heavily, resting his chin atop her head.

Jada groaned. "Let's not talk about it. Just enjoy it."

"I can do that." He pulled back and tilted her head for an explosive kiss that seemed to last for hours, melting her resolve and tingling her toes. "I came six hours for that, man. You look too good for me to resist." He ran his thumb over her bottom lip, his eyes fastened on it. "Was that too fast?"

Jada pulled away, grabbing his hand and leading him into the living room. "I mean, it was just a kiss. Plus, we've been talking every day, and it's not like you're spending the night with me or anything. I like the tempo."

She was afraid to tell him that she had thoroughly enjoyed it and hoped it would happen again and again all weekend long, but she didn't want to come on too strong, or bite off more than she could chew right now. Plus, her mother's words echoed in her mind, *a man won't be too quick to buy the cow if he can get the milk for free.* She didn't want him to think of her as being desperate or hard-up for attention, so she decided to play it cool.

She plopped on the couch, and he followed her, pulling her feet into his lap. Jada knew that she should feel uneasy, being that she had only known him for a month, but she felt oddly comfortable with him. Every day that she had spoken to him, he offered words of encouragement and support, a male companionship and intellectual perspective that she had missed. He was patient and gentle, and she had already discovered that he was much more emotionally available than she was, a fact that had unnerved her, but they had agreed to take things as slow as possible. While he had expressed his desire to be exclusive, he seemed understanding when she told him that she just wasn't ready for that level of commitment; so, they had agreed to casually date for the time being. She liked knowing that there wasn't any pressure on her to be the perfect host, girlfriend, or wife-to-be.

She'd spent three years trying to convince Caleb that she was deserving of the title and willing to stand alongside him through thick and thin, and it still hadn't panned out as she'd hoped, but now, she was discovering the mistakes she'd made and exploring this newfound woman that she thoroughly enjoyed, one that was hardworking, sincere, determined, and ambitious. And even more, she loved that none of those qualities seemed to threaten Johnathan. In fact, he seemed to be even more driven than she, which made him even more attractive and hard to resist. *Get yourself in check, Jay,* she thought. She stared at his lips, perfectly framed by a low-cut beard. She loved the soft stubble along his jaw line and the way it faded into his low haircut. There was no doubt in her mind that she was highly attracted to him. She attempted to blink the thoughts out of her head, tuning back into their conversation.

"I'm just making sure you're comfortable with all this." He looked around the room, fumbling with one of the decorative couch pillows. "You have a nice place. It's very you with all of the sultry colors with spots of brightness and stuff. I see you everywhere." He patted her leg softly.

She chuckled and followed his gaze to the hand-painted Akanian vase that her former professor had bought her as a souvenir from Ghana.

"That's beautiful."

"Yeah. I think so, too. On the other side, there's the word 'Sankofa,' which basically means 'return and take it'."

"Wow. That's neat." He chuckled. "What exactly does it mean?"

"Well," she smiled. "It means not to be afraid to accept lessons and learn from your past. In learning from and exploring the past, you can go back and reclaim the things that are rightfully yours."

"Deep stuff." He laced his fingers in hers. "Are you still there?" He looked at her with downcast eyes, his long eyelashes fanning his muscular cheek.

"Am I where?" She stared back in confusion.

"Still in the past. I know you want us to move slowly, but I don't want to feel as though you are stringing me along either." He cupped her hand in his, staring back at her intensely.

"I can't sit here and say that I am one hundred percent over him; I devoted almost four years of my life to him, so it takes time. But as far as stringing you along, I wouldn't do that, which is why I am not asking for an exclusive relationship with you. I enjoy talking to you, and you are so sure of yourself. Your hustle matches mine, and I dig that; however, I can understand if you need something more from someone else more willing to commit to you right now." She held her breathe as he looked her over, searching her face for what she presumed to be sincerity.

"Whew!" He heaved a long sigh of relief, catching her off guard. "I really was scared to ask you that. Man, I was afraid of your answer, but being that I've already driven six hours, what could I have done?" He chuckled, resting one arm behind his head and his hand on his flat torso. Finally, he looked over at her. "I'm willing to go your speed." He squeezed her leg gently. "I'm going to win you over." His eyes twinkled with challenge as he leaned towards her.

"You up for the challenge?" His face was mere inches from hers. He tucked an escaped strand of hair behind her ear, his fingers making a trail down her neck and across her collarbone.

She shivered under his touch. "Absolutely," she drawled, winking back at him and returning his gaze.

He yanked her body against his. His hand fanned the small of her back, as he seized her lips in a fiery kiss. *This weekend is going to be entirely too short*, she thought as he nibbled along her bottom lip.

***

Jada seemed to skip to the entrance, smirking with thoughts of her and Johnathan's weekend. They'd gone to the movies, played laser tag, and even visited a museum in a nearby city. She knew the lack of sleep would hit her like a ton of bricks by lunchtime, but for the time-being, she would relish in the sense of rejuvenation she now felt walking into the school building. She nodded and waved at many of her colleagues as she passed their classrooms. Everyone seemed to be lagging around, unhappy about being back at work. Mr. Oliver, the janitor, tipped his baseball cap at her before giving her a toothless grin.

"Say girl, you look like you had a good break!" He winked at her.

"Sure did, Mr. Oliver!" She smiled back. "How about you?"

"Oh, Child. What break? I came up here and waxed these floors and all." He took his hat off and scratched the top of his head. "Us minimum wage folks don't get no break like everybody else. We still needs our checks."

Jada sobered, upset that she hadn't considered him and the others. "But Mr. Oliver, you've been here for years. You only make minimum wage?"

"Sho' nuff!" He placed a hefty amount of chewing tobacco in his cheek. "They ain't bout helping us too much."

"That's a shame." Jada shifted from foot to foot, uncomfortable with what she was hearing. "No bonus or anything?"

"Not a thing." He pulled his old flip phone from his back pocket, checking the time. "But I'm hanging in here 'til I can't hang no mo'. Complaining don't get you nowhere 'round here."

"I've noticed that since being here, Mr. Oliver."

"Well, you gon' keep on noticing it, girl. This place'll eat you up if you let it." He pushed the mop and bucket down the hall while whistling, leaving her in the middle of the lunch hall.

The bell sounded loudly, and energetic students filtered into the building. Jada placed her index finger alongside her temple as a sharp pain rippled through her head. *It's gonna be a long day*, she thought.

***

"Ms. H., your boy Ashton's in the office." Demetria peeked in, smacked the door, and hurried down the hall.

Jada snatched her keys off her desk and shuffled out of the room, locking the door behind her. Other than the time that she'd ran into Ashton working at Bargain Foods, the new store in the area, she hadn't seen or heard about him. He'd smiled, and his words stumbled out rapidly, but she could tell that it was all a disguise by the way that he continuously scratched his chin and avoided eye contact with her. She'd given him her personal email address and told him to contact her if he needed her. He'd promised he would, but she hadn't heard from him. She couldn't help but remember his last words: "I gotta do what I gotta do, Ms. H. My pops say that if I don't work, I don't eat." Jada saw the flag of surrender as his words settled in the air. She'd refused to accept it. In the three weeks since she'd returned from Spring Break, she'd spoken to Mr. Rucker about him and even called the Superintendent's office; the closest she'd gotten to any resolution was scheduling a meeting with the Assistant Superintendent in two weeks. However, she couldn't help but feel that she'd already lost the battle since Ashton's parents weren't on board and to add insult to injury, Ms. Calloway was the Assistant Superintendent's sister, a fact that his secretary had reminded her

208

about before suggesting, "Have you tried asking Ms. Calloway to bring it up to him? That will really bring some results."

Jada had blown hard into the receiver. "No, I'll just meet with him." Now, she had an inkling as to how Mrs. Kimble and Ms. Henson had escaped scrutiny amid the school sex scandal.

Now, as she half jogged, half skipped to the office, she wasn't sure what she would do or say, but she marched on. She could see Ashton through the glass window in the middle of the door. His coloring was rising as he gestured dramatically while speaking to Mr. Rucker.

Jada pushed open the door and stepped into the dim office. Ashton stopped talking and looked helplessly in her direction.

"Ms. Harris, can I help you?" Mr. Rucker asked in an irritated voice, scratching his head vigorously.

Jada ignored him and looked to Ashton for an explanation.

"Ms. Harris, I'm trying to get back in school. I really need to come back. I won't get in any more trouble or goof around. This working-everyday-thing is just not for me, Ms. H. Tell him; tell him I'm not a bad kid." His eyes pleaded with her.

Her breathe caught in her throat at the desperation with which he'd spoken. There was no doubt that he'd meant every word. "H-he's not a bad kid, Mr. Rucker. The mere fact that he is here right now is enough to say that he truly wants to be here. He doesn't have any kind of criminal record or anything."

"I get that, Ms. Harris." He ran his hand through his hair and down his face slowly. "You are but one teacher. Other teachers don't have the same experiences with Mr. Gross. Plus, if I allow him back, I have to do the same for other students."

"We're not talking about other students right now, Mr. Rucker." she hissed calmly, her hand clenching by her side. "I can assure you that you won't be making a mistake. Part of being a well-rounded principal is compassion and second chances. Here's your chance to really make a difference and show this young man that you are willing to take a risk for his success. You cannot let him walk back out of the door. That's just not the way to go."

He shifted his weight from one foot to the other. He turned to Ms. Allen, who had been quietly listening to the whole exchange while peeking ever-so-often over her hot pink glasses. "Ms. Allen, do you mind calling Mrs. Barnes to the office?"

"Sure." She dialed Mrs. Barnes' room number.

Mr. Rucker turned back to Jada and Ashton. "I can't in good faith allow you back into the school without clearing it with Mrs. Barnes, whose referral slip resulted in your expulsion. I think that's fair."

"Fair?" Jada scoffed, but she bit her tongue, not wanting to discourage Ashton. She stepped closer to him and gave his hand a quick squeeze as they waited for Mrs. Barnes.

When Mrs. Barnes entered the office, a look of confusion and then boredom spread across her face. "May I know why I was summoned here? I thought he," she waved in Ashton's direction "was expelled."

Mr. Rucker shoved his hands in his pockets. "He is, Mrs. Barnes, but Ashton, here, came to ask me to reconsider his suspension. I felt that it is only right for you to weigh in, as I know he and you had many run-ins."

She seemed to be genuinely surprised and possibly even pleased by the principal's words. "W-w-why, yes. Well, you are correct that Ashton and I have never seen eye-to-eye in my classroom. And Ashton, I appreciate your courage in coming here and begging to come back."

Begging? Jada fumed. She couldn't believe that he was entrusting Ashton's future in the hands of this buffoon. *God, please, please change this woman's heart. Make her find favor in him even though she doesn't want to,* she prayed silently.

"I think it says a lot about you" she continued, "but to be frank, I don't feel safe having you in my class. It's always a head-on collision with you."

"Wait a minute." Jada was unable to remain quiet any longer. "You wrote him up for goofing around, using profanity, and disagreeing with you. How, then, does that become 'feeling unsafe'? He didn't threaten you or assault you in any way. This is ridiculous." She looked to Mr. Rucker for reassurance. His face was blank.

Mrs. Barnes smirked at her. "While, no, he didn't physically assault me, I'm not sure if you know it or not, but words are just as hurtful as fists. How long before he tired of verbally assaulting me and resorted to physical abuse? Are you aware that I've written him up almost 8 times this year?"

"You've got to be kidding me! At what point do you look at what *you* could be doing that makes him respond to you that way? I'm not condoning his actions, and it is wrong for him to call you out of your name, but he is a child. Didn't you make mistakes as a child? How do you call yourself a teacher with that mindset?"

"That's easy. I look at my degrees and experiences, which far exceed yours, and you know what all of that tells me?" She cocked her head to the side and placed her index finger under her chin. "It tells me that I know my students, and my main goal is to protect the class environment. Mr. Gross is a detriment to that space. So I'm sorry but no." She turned back to Mr. Rucker, her fingers intertwined below her hanging stomach and her usually pale cheeks glistening with red color. "If there is nothing else, Mr. Rucker…"

"Ah, yes, Mrs. Barnes, you may leave." She sauntered out of the room, her pointy nose a bit higher in the air than it had been before.

"So, what now?" Ashton's shoulders hung in defeat as he stared back at the principal.

"I'm sorry, son. There's really nothing I can do."

Jada shook her head. "What do you mean? She said that *she* didn't feel safe with him in *her* classroom; she never said that he is a danger to the school as a whole. What about taking him out of her class?"

"She is the only Spanish teacher. He needs those credits. There really isn't anything I can do, but Mr. Gross, come back and we'll kick next year off right." He extended his hand to the somber-faced boy.

Ashton slowly raised his head to make eye contact with him. "I came in here trying to talk you into letting me back in, and all you can say is come back next year?! Then, you want me to shake your freaking hand?! Nah, man." He shook his head slowly, balling his hands into fists by his side. "I'll never step foot back in this hell hole that ya'll call a school. Everybody I know itching to get away from this junt, and here I am running back to it like a fool."He snatched his backpack from the floor and stormed out of the office.

Jada ran after him. "Ashton, Ashton, wait" she called. She caught up to him and grabbed his shoulder. "It doesn't have to end here. We can keep fighting for you."

"Ms. H, I appreciate your help, but I wouldn't want to come back here. For what? For them to just look for reasons to get rid of me again? Nah, it's just like they say, this white folk's land. *We* just here surviving. That's what ima do. Survive this bullcrap."

"Ashton, it's more to life than just surviving. You gotta know that."

"No, not for everybody, Ms. H. But look I gotta go. I'll see you around." He held his fist out to her. She hesitantly bumped hers against his. He smiled at her before tugging his backpack on his shoulder and walking slowly across the parking lot. She watched him walk until he was out of sight at which time she wiped the tears from her cheek. She was genuinely afraid for him and all the other Ashtons that would enter the school.

Walking back into the building, she felt defeated. Ms. Allen approached her with a few tissues and tiny smile. "Girl, you can't get too attached to these students. It'll leave you disappointed every time."

She blew into the tissue and walked back to her classroom. *God, please tell me what to do.*

Chapter Seventeen

"The brutally murdered male found shot to death in a wooden part of DeFlore County has been identified as 15-year-old Ashton Gross."

The news reporter's words coursed through Jada's spine. She braced herself against the mirror, blankly staring at the reflection of the television. A smiling picture of Ashton sat in the middle of the screen looking back at her. She wasn't sure when the tears began, but she was unable to stop them. They flowed and flowed as her shoulders shook uncontrollably until she was slumped over on the hardwood floor.

The news reporter continued, "The text messages found on his phone lead investigators to believe that he was killed over a drug deal gone bad. Ashton Gross's name might sound familiar to you in that he was a former breakout basketball and football star at Caldwin

High School. A vigil is set to be held for him in the near future. Details are forthcoming."

A guttural sob seeped from her suddenly. She lay on her side and curled into a fetal position, unable to think of anything more than her last time speaking to him. She knew she should be getting ready for work, but this news made everything seem unnecessary and out of her control. She was supposed to meet with the Assistant Superintendent today, and now, she couldn't see any reason to even go to school; she cried harder as she thought about the effect this news would have on all of her students. She dragged herself off of the floor and tucked her arms into her suit jacket. She moved slowly from room to room as if in a daze, thoughts of her students pushing her forward.

***

The air stood still in the school. Loud sniffles and moans echoed throughout the gym. Jada knew she was walking, but the floor felt like air under her feet. She seemed to be floating around the room, hearing some students recount fond memories of Ashton, others wondering why they even showed up for school, and still some taking pictures with sad faces, crying emoji, and heart-shaped hands, and she floated away, up far away from all the chatter and crying to a shrill shriek. It didn't sound like it would end. She looked about the room, but there was only darkness, a midnight blue hole and screaming. But there was no one there. Then, she turned to her right, and she saw a very small version of herself standing there, surrounded by darkness, and she knew where it had come from. Her outward, stoic expression was shattered by a well of tears that gathered in her lower lid and began to spill down her cheeks. She felt her soul being squeezed from her body and turned to find Demetria there, enveloping her in a tight embrace.

Jada patted her arm, the girl's tears wetting her shirt. "It's alright, sweetheart. It's alright." She felt stupid saying it, but what more could she say? A large number of her freshman students surrounded her, all crying and whispering words of encouragement to each other until Mr. Rucker entered the room.

He tapped the microphone sharply. "Good morning, everyone." He cleared his throat, looking as if he was carefully considering his next words. "I know that all of you have heard about As--" He stopped suddenly, loosening his tie. "Ashton Gross. It is such a tragedy that we lost him this way. I know that each of you can remember him fondly. I hope that you know that if you need to talk, Ms. Henson, our counselor, will be more than happy to speak with you."

"Who can we talk to about you?!" A boy named Anthony yelled, standing up and pointing his finger accusingly at Mr. Rucker. "Ain't you the reason he was in those streets in the first place?"

A chorus of chatter and applause sounded around the gym. Mr. Rucker cleared his throat again, "N-n-now, I know you all are angry, but we must remember why w--"

"Nah. We gotta remember our homie. The one you threw in the streets!" Jose yelled, tears canvasing his face. He stood, facing the small-looking man. "He was our brother! You just as guilty as the fools who killed him!" He snatched his hood on his head and turned to those seated behind him. "Our brother would still be alive if not for him!" His statement was met with loud applause, dog whistles, and heavy stomps that filled the room.

Mr. Rucker attempted to speak but to no avail. The students continued to chant and clap. In defeat, he rested his arms by his sides and looked to the faculty helplessly.

Jada looked about the room in amazement, unable to believe what she was witnessing. The students were angry, deeply wounded, and stunned by the loss. She felt ashamed that she hadn't considered just how significant Ashton's death would mean to them, classmates he had known since Kindergarten. This realization seemed to sober her up; she slowly pulled away from the heap of students surrounding her and walked towards Ms. Henson, the counselor.

She spoke to her quietly through gritted teeth. "Look, you've been here longer than me so you know most of the students. Plus your credentials say that you are better at this than me. You need to speak to them. They'll listen to you." She registered the hesitation that flashed across the woman's face. "Considering the low-down stuff that you have been a part of here, it is the very least that you can do." She climbed the stairs back into the bleachers and sat amidst the students, speaking words of encouragement to each of them.

She looked up at the sound of Ms. Henson's voice vibrating from the speakers. "Hi, Family." She looked about the room. "First, let me start by saying that I am so sorry for all of your loss. Ashton was a bright, young man that we all loved so much. So trust me when I say that I feel your pain. I really do, and you are going to feel that." She wiped a fallen tear from her chin. "Right now, I know that your emotions are high, but this is not the time to point fingers. We *must* take the time to remember Ashton. Can we do that?" She offered the crowd a half-smile, taking the time to visually survey the room. The chatter had ceased, and the students seemed to hang on to every word. "Good. Now, I would like for ten of you to step up to the mic and share your fondest memory of Ashton. While they're doing that, teachers I need you all positioned around the room so that you can support them however they need it." The teachers began to move about. Jada stayed seated, squeezing students' hands tighter. Roughly twenty students ran down to line up.

She passed the microphone to Anthony, the first student in the line. He fidgeted for a minute but seemed calmer when Luiz placed his hand on his shoulder.

Jada watched them through blurry eyes, knowing that while they were hurting, they were more united than she had ever seen them.

***

Roughly two hours later and the students spilled out of the gym into their third period classes. They seemed to be less aggressive than they'd been at the start of the school day. Jada knew that she had Ms. Henson to thank for that. Thanks to her, the assembly had turned into a positive and sensitive two hours remembering Ashton's life with the students sharing mostly funny moments from their childhood. While there had still been some crying, they seemed to be genuinely appreciative for the opportunity to share their experiences.

Jada spotted Ms. Henson among the crowd and tapped her on the shoulder. She turned quickly.

"Hey. I just want to thank you for giving them a space for expression. I know they really appreciate it, too."

"I'm just glad you trusted me to do it." She smiled back at her. "Why didn't someone tell me about everything between Ashton and Mrs. Barnes?"

Jada cocked her head in confusion. "I was under the impression that you knew. He told me he'd spoken to you about it but that you'd said there was nothing you could do."

She seemed to dip her head in shame. "I-I actually did say that. But I had no idea he'd come up to the school for re-entry. I really wish *you'd* told me."

"I really didn't think about it. I guess because you and I haven't talked since all of that stuff with Mr. Dennis. I just didn't think there was anything anyone could do. I actually had a meeting scheduled with the Assistant Superintendent for today. Too little, too late I guess."

The grabbed her arm softly. "Look, just like these students, you can't beat yourself up over this. You did all that you could." She squeezed her arm lightly, gave a little smile, and pranced towards her office.

But what if I didn't do all that I could? She wondered, walking slowly behind the students towards her classroom.

Chapter *Eighteen*

Johnathan held her tightly around her waist. "How are you doing, babe?" He asked softly.

She looked up at him. "I'm making it." She closed the door behind him and followed him into the living room.

"You know I wish I could've gotten here sooner. I could tell you needed a shoulder to lean on. I'm so sorry, baby." He pulled her down to the couch and tucked his arm around her, tugging her close to his side.

She relished in in his scent and the warmth generating from his body. "I know, but I had my family. They've been very attentive." She snuggled closer to him.

He heaved a long sigh. "That's great. I didn't like the way you'd been sounding on the phone. I had to see you."

"Yeah, but I'm fine, though. I promise." She peeked up at him with a serious look.

He suddenly moved away from her. "Look, I need you to stop that."

"Stop what?" Confusion registered on her face.

"Saying that you're fine. You've been telling me that all week." He ran his hand over his sleek hair in frustration. "It's okay not to be alright. I need you to know that. At some point, if we're going to continue whatever it is that we're doing, I need for you to understand that it is okay for you not to be okay around me."

Jada watched his jaw muscles flex, a sign that he was slightly annoyed. "I'm not trying to force you to warm up to me, but I really like you, man. I really do. All I could think about this week was getting to you because your voice wasn't your own. You didn't laugh at any of my lame jokes. You weren't even eating. I didn't like hearing it or feeling helpless to it, but I'm here now. Tell me what you need."

"I need you to leave." She spoke softly as if fearful of the impact her words would have on him. She stood and began to walk towards the door. Surprisingly, he didn't move from the couch.

"You don't need me to leave." He cupped his hands beneath his chin. "I feel that you're trying to distance yourself from me now because you feel what I said."

"N-no, I really just need some space, Johnathan." She stood in the archway, her arms folded stubbornly over her chest.

"I drove six hours. I'm not going anywhere. Now, you can sit down and talk to me or you can find the space you say you need somewhere else in this beautifully, decorated, spacious house," he said sarcastically, crossing his arms behind his head and stretching his long legs towards her pearl shag rug.

Not sure what to do, she stood in the hall, biting one side of her lip, and fidgeting with the bracelet on her arm. He seemed to be ignoring her, unbothered by her reluctance to join him on the couch. He looked relaxed with his eyes closed and his smooth stomach moving up and down slowly. He looked to be fast asleep.

She walked into the living room and slowly sank into the open space beside him, watching his every move.

He suddenly sat up, pulled her onto his lap, and kissed her with passion that brought tears to her eyes. He wrapped his arms around her tightly and nuzzled her neck with his beard. "I love everything about you," he whispered. "Your curves, your smile, your independence, your laugh when you are the only one that thinks something is funny, and even your stubbornness at times. But you know what I find absolutely intriguing about you," he paused slightly, kissing her ear. "I love how much you care about your students. I can only pray for someone like you to be the mother of my future children. Do you hear me?"

Jada nodded as her tears fell to his crisp white shirt.

"I'm here for you, baby." He crooned in her ear as her sniffles turned into low sobs that she'd contained the whole week. Her body shook with the release, and he was there accompanying every sob with an affectionate touch or words of endearment. Jada didn't remember falling asleep in his arms.

***

Today was the day. A month after the school had been rocked by tragedy and Ashton's funeral, and everything seemed to be operating as normal. She practiced the words she'd say to the Assistant Superintendent in reference to the school's policy about student discipline. Walking into the conference room, she felt confident that she would be heard.

Ms. Allen greeted her and placed a pitcher of water in the middle of the table. The Assistant Superintendent, Mr. Ward, followed her into the room. His red suit jacket was freshly steamed and crisp, the blue stitching flashing under the fluorescent light. Jada could tell from his perfect coils and creased navy blue pants that he took great pride in his appearance. She shouldn't have expected anything different from the brother of Ms. Calloway.

"Good morning, Ms. Harris," he boomed.

"Hi, Mr. Ward," she stood and shook his extended hand. "I'm so glad that during this tragic time you were able to meet with me."

"Oh, it's nothing." He rolled up his sleeves and pulled his pen from behind his ear. "I understand that we are here about the school discipline here. How can I help you?"

"Well, as you know the students have been rocked by Ashton Gross's recent death." He nodded in acknowledgement. "While I'm not condoning what he was doing, I know that it, for Ashton, might have resembled a last resort. We're talking about a kid who absolutely loves-- I mean loved---school. And so many people loved him, including me. When Ashton came back to the school two weeks before he was murdered, he was practically begging Mr. Rucker to allow him to re-enroll. In the end, Mr. Rucker left the decision up to Mrs. Barnes, a woman who refuses to identify with many of the black children. I believe that the disciplinary system needs to change. Before principals even consider expelling a student, they should be required to show that the student is a threat to those around him from multiple perspectives, not just one heavily biased perception. It just isn't fair." She took a breath.

"I see." He continued to scribble on his notepad. "I think what we're seeing here is not a problem with the policy but rather with the administrator."

"Well, not exactly. I believe it's both. There must be some sort of policy in place that will guide all principals in the school. You know, something that keeps them all on one accord."

"Well, I can't make any promises right now, Ms. Harris, but I can tell you that I will bring it up with Superintendent House." He began to gather his belongings from the long wooden table.

"When will I hear something?" She felt that she was losing ground. She expected more, something more definite.

"I will be in touch by the end of the week." He stood. "But I'm going to let you in on a little secret. Mr. Rucker will not return as the principal of *this* school next year." He looked at her expectantly.

"W-wow. Who will take his position?"

"We've found someone with more experience that we're considering trying out." He walked towards the door. Jada hurried behind him.

"But you said *this* school. Where is he going?"

"Ahh, he'll move to another school in the district."

"B-but---" she scratched her chin. "that defeats the----."

"You can't win it all at once, Ms. Harris. I'll be in touch." He nodded and was gone as quick as he'd come.

The sound of glass bumping glass caught her attention. She turned to find Mr. Rucker stiffly leaning over a cardboard box, piling his belongings on top of each other. He met her gaze and held it, an accusatory glaze flashed over them. She looked away and walked quickly back to her classroom.

Notes from her students flanked her door and several boxes lined the walls. One by one she began to lug the boxes to her car, running into a group of students who volunteered to help. After helping them load the boxes and line the hallway with the desks, she stood in the middle of her empty room, not sure how to feel. She spun around and a lone piece of paper on her desk caught her attention. She walked over to it and picked up the past due contract. She folded it up in her hand, locked the door, and walked to the office.

"Ms. Allen, I came to drop off my key and this." She waved the folded paper in her hand but paused before giving it to Ms. Allen. She pulled the pen from behind her ear and stared at the paper for a while. Ms. Allen stood by silently.

She slowly signed her name along the dotted line, committing herself to another year at Caldwin High, and she had no reason why, other than a chance at doing it better next year.

"I'm glad you're coming back," Ms. Allen beamed.

Jada offered a stiff nod, smacked the counter, and pulled her cellphone out of her pocket. She hadn't even taught for a full year yet, and she welcomed the summer with open arms.

Until next time, Caldwin, she thought as she pulled her sunglasses down over glistening eyes and dialed Johnathan. He answered on the second ring.

"Uh-oh, do I smell freedom?" He chuckled into the phone.

Jada found herself giggling. "Yep, a whole bunch of it." She readjusted the rearview mirror and steered her car onto the freeway towards Atlanta.

TALES OF A FIRST-YEAR TEACHER: PART ONE

Words from the Author

First, I would like to thank you for devoting a portion of your time to reading my novel. I hope that you enjoyed following Jada on her journey as a plus-size, Black woman and developing first-year teacher because, her journey is not over. In case you hadn't noticed, she is only six months into her first year of teaching within the public school system. Thus, I anticipate your continued dedication in readership as we see the intersections at which she arrives and the continued battles she must encounter. While at the offset, this novel appears to be a chronicling of the black love, educational, and professional experiences of one woman, my goal was to provide insight into the lives, minds, cultures, and practices of the school personnel and educational settings in which we entrust the care of our children, especially our young, impressionable, and rather vulnerable Black children. When I began drafting my thoughts for this novel, I pondered on the best way to effectively communicate many of the hardships and decisions experienced by those in the buildings we call schools while, simultaneously, creating a space for school stakeholders (you, you, and you) to engage in thought-provoking and transparent dialogue about what happens in our schools. Hence, we see Jada grappling with her personal and professional life in ways that leave her questioning, critiquing, and unpacking parts of herself, a task that can be quite daunting to complete alone. However, WE must do the work, for the sake of our children and their children. I encourage you to ask yourself, first, and then others within your personal _and_ professional circles the following questions for discussion:

1. What inherent biases, if any, do _I_ bring to both personal and professional settings?
2. If applicable, what experiences or teachings are at the foundation of those biases?
3. How have _I_ witnessed, experienced, or demonstrated these biases in both my personal and/or professional settings?
4. In what ways, if any, have _I_ been disappointed by someone _I_ initially admired?
5. In what ways, if any, have _I_ managed to disappoint someone who admired me?
6. What role does silence play in both effective and ineffective leadership and relationships?
7. If I had to list my 5 identifiers, they would be: __________________. Explain.
8. What qualities do I expect from others, and how do I intend to identify them?
9. Who holds power in our society and whom does this power work to subjugate?
10. What role does both subjugation and power have on 1) the oppressor, 2) the oppressed, and 3) the global society?

11. What is my purpose, and do I function in a capacity that
adheres to this purpose?

You may discuss all off these questions in relation to the novel.
Once again, thank you for reading and be sure to look out for part
two of *Tales of a First Year Teacher*.

Abundant Love & Blessings,

J.D.

ABOUT THE AUTHOR

Born in Chicago, IL and raised in North Mississippi, J.D. Parks has been a strong advocate for social justice education; she believes in providing safe spaces for those who are typically silenced such as minority people, students, and teachers. Hence, she enjoys exploring and combining the lived experiences of under-privileged and under-represented people in cross-genre fiction. J.D. has served as a high school English teacher and is currently an English professor at a Historically Black College & University (HBCU) located in the Mid-South. When she's not writing, reading, or performing both simultaneously, she is relaxing with her family Fridays and sipping from a tall glass of strawberry lemonade.